Beethoven Conf

AND

Brahms Gets I

Beethoven Confidential

KEN RUSSELL

AND

JO ANDERSON

AND

Brahms Gets Laid

KEN RUSSELL

PETER OWEN

LONDON AND CHESTER SPRINGS, PA, USA

PETER OWEN PUBLISHERS
73 Kenway Road
London SW5 ORE

Peter Owen books are distributed in the USA by
Dufour Editions Inc., Chester Springs, PA 19425-0007

First published in Great Britain by Peter Owen Publishers 2007

ISBN 978 0 7206 1279 0

A catalogue record for this book is available from the British Library

Printed and bound in Great Britain by
Windsor Print Production Ltd, Tonbridge, Kent

For Elize

Preface

BEETHOVEN CONFIDENTIAL STARTED life as a play by my co-author Jo Anderson, a talented author/actor who sent it to me proposing we turn her work of art into a screenplay. Inspired by her fascinating treatment of the subject in terms of drama and humour, I was also intrigued by the story of the rivalry between two would-be biographers in the quest for the 'Immortal Beloved' – Beethoven's secret love. It was a wonderful whodunit or, to be more precise, 'whowasit'.

In next to no time we had produced a script, found a producer, our German locations and our cast – which included Jodie Foster, Glenda Jackson and Anthony Hopkins as the deaf genius. The only thing we did not find was the money – so the film was never made. Disaster, horror, tragedy – two years' work for nothing!

But such an original conception about one of the greatest musical geniuses of all time was too good to waste, so here it is in print – one of the most bizarre and compelling detective yarns of all time. And here we have not one private eye but two – personal friends of Beethoven, pitted against each other in a race to reveal the mystery they still say could never be solved. And they were right – until now.

Of course Bach, Beethoven and Brahms, the three big names in classical music today are the same as they were well over a century ago, and so far there are no signs of any change in that great triumvirate, though Brahms was also renowned for three Bs of his own – beer, beard and belly.

Tradition has it that he died a confirmed bachelor and a respected pillar of society, who liked nothing better than a pint at the local after an evening of music-making and a walk through the Black Forest at weekends with his mates. And he was kind to his mum, respectful of his dad and probably one of the most reliable baby-sitters of all time.

But what of his sex life? What sex life? Surely this cosy old soul was above such stuff as babies are made of? Really? Have you listened to his music? Agreed, the *Academic Festival Overture* paints a picture of the beer-swilling Brahms, full of student bonhomie, whom we have come to know and love, but take a listen to the inner movements of his Third Symphony for a sensuality that is hard to beat. If it's white hot passion you're after, try the opening of the First Symphony and tell me if that doesn't have balls. And surely there's a section in the Fourth that can only be the sex act set to music.

Brahms probably knew more about sex than any composer before or since. After all, he was born in the red-light district of Hamburg and spent his formative years playing honky-tonk piano in every whorehouse in town. Well, not all of them, perhaps, but he certainly knew his way around.

This knowledge set me thinking, as did my investigation into his close association with that insane genius of the keyboard Robert Schumann and his psychologically disturbed wife and kids. So hold on to your hats for the sex romp of the (nineteenth) century.

Beethoven Confidential

Contents

BEETHOVEN CONFIDENTIAL

ONE

The Skull

*B*EETHOVEN, DRAPED IN a sheet, lies dead on a piano. He is surrounded by the shambles in which he perpetually lived. Frugal furniture, shabby curtains, a rickety four-poster, crates of wine, boxes of manuscript paper and piles of clothing. The place suggests a junk shop rather than a respectable apartment in the tenement where the composer spent his last remaining days.

Dr Warwuch, an elderly and highly respected physician, is preparing for the autopsy. He will shortly be making an incision above Beethoven's left ear. But first the head must be shaved, and he sharpens a razor.

Near by, Danhauser, a round-shouldered little man, and his skeletal assistant Tantfl are stirring a mixture from which the death mask will be made. Danhauser regards Dr Warwuch with mistrust.

'Don't mess him up too much or they'll never recognize him,' he urges. 'I've seen your autopsies before.'

'I am about to probe the secret of his genius for the benefit of humanity,' proclaims Dr Warwuch. 'You are about to create a superficial effigy for the morbid to gape at in some tawdry waxworks for the benefit of your own pocket. Pray desist.'

While Danhauser scowls and stirs his plaster more violently a dapper little man whom it transpires is an auctioneer politely takes the razor out of the doctor's hand, examines the blade and turns to his bespectacled assistant who is cataloguing the effects.

'Item: one razor, finest Ruhr steel, property Ludwig van Beethoven. Actually used to shave the deceased.' He returns it to the doctor. 'Not absolutely essential. You clean it after use. Thank you, doctor.'

His assistant hands the auctioneer a dog-eared notebook.

'There are twenty-six of these, sir, full of scribble. Shall I dispose of them in one lot?'

'Good heavens, no,' exclaims the auctioneer. 'Conversation books, valuable items – proof he was deaf.' He moves on, pecking through the jumble like a magpie while two shadowy figures creep around the room hissing and whispering conspiratorially. They appear to be searching for something; through bookshelves, under carpets, beneath cushions, behind pictures, in desks and drawers and through piles of manuscripts. They ransack everything neatly but methodically. They are not thieves but friends of Beethoven's though not of each other, which soon becomes evident, as does the object of their search. Anton Schindler, middle-aged, tall, spectral and opinionated, regards himself as Beethoven's official biographer and is jealous of Karl Holtz not only for the fact that he is good-looking and twenty years younger but also for the more intimate relationship he enjoyed with the composer.

'Perhaps he deposited them at the bank. That would be the logical thing to do,' whispers Schindler.

'Then that's the last place we should look,' mutters Holtz. 'Have you looked in his shoes?'

'Of course not!' snaps Schindler.

'He was forever stuffing them with anything that came to hand to try to keep out the wet,' explains Holtz. 'I'll never forget the night he was to conduct the première of the Seventh Symphony. Couldn't find the Finale anywhere. We turned the place upside down. Nowhere! Until the maidservant found it tucked in his shoe.'

Schindler is envious that he did not witness the scene himself. 'Ah, but do you know *which* shoe?'

'Left foot, right foot, what does it signify?'

'Everything about Beethoven is significant,' retorts Schindler.

'Even his whores?' asks Holtz sarcastically. 'Will you touch on *their* significance in your "official biography", Herr Schindler?'

'What possible relevance could they have to his art?'

'I suppose it depends on their pedigree.'

Schindler can sense trouble brewing and continues the search next door in the bedroom, followed by Holtz, who enjoys ribbing him. 'Will you mention Countess Erdody, for instance?'

'Of course,' says Schindler loftily.

'And Elsa Schmitt – will you mention her?'

'That trollop. Certainly not! How can you even ask?' replies Schindler in disgust.

'They were both very close to Beethoven,' says Holtz with a shrug. 'One lived in a palace, the other in a brothel, that's all.'

'Eureka!' shouts Schindler triumphantly as a loose nail he has been fiddling with on the writing desk comes away in his hand, releasing a secret drawer that drops on to the floor scattering its contents at the feet of the two startled rivals.

As Schindler makes a dive for the prize, a pile of valuable bank shares, Holtz kneels at his side and picks up an assortment of papers covered in scribbled pencil. Schindler makes a grab for them, but Holtz swiftly whisks them out of his reach.

'What have you there?' hisses Schindler. 'Those papers may be of a private nature.'

'Then who better than an old friend to peruse them first?' says Holtz, backing away. 'They may be unfit for publication.'

'Let me be the judge of that.'

'I'd rather turn them over to the auctioneer!' Holtz calls over his shoulder through to the next room, 'Is the auctioneer there?'

Danhauser looks up from his bucket of plaster and replies, 'Gone to lunch.'

'No, please, no,' begs Schindler, following Holtz into the room.

'For God's sake calm down, man,' urges Holtz. 'It would be foolish in the extreme for us to cross swords over what might transpire to be nothing but a shopping list.' Even so he crouches against the wall to prevent the envious Schindler from looking over his shoulder, his eyes racing over the papers.

'A scrap of trivia in a secret drawer. What nonsense!' scoffs Schindler.

'Trivia, eh? Everything is significant – except sex, yes?' says Holtz, moving rapidly away from Schindler, who quickly follows him. 'Listen to this!

> ... my Angel, my all, my very self ... why this deep sorrow when necessity speaks – can our love endure except through sacrifices? Through not demanding everything from one another; can you change the fact that you are not wholly mine, I not wholly yours. We shall surely see each other again soon ... my heart is full of so many things to say to you – ah – there are moments

when I feel that speech amounts to nothing at all – cheer up – remain my true, my only treasure, my all as I am yours.

Your faithful Ludwig

'What do you make of that?' As Holtz comes to a halt and turns on him, the gangling Schindler snatches the letter away and scrutinizes it for clues.

'No address, no name. Just Monday 6 July – damn it, not even the year. The man's impossible! Now we shall never know her identity. I wonder why he never sent it.'

'Of course he sent it,' argues Holtz. 'This must be a rough copy or a first draft. It's extraordinary, Schindler. In all the years of our acquaintance I never knew him to express himself as strongly as this about anything – certainly not a woman, and he knew quite a few in his time.'

But Schindler has just caught sight of the doctor shaving Beethoven's skull and is momentarily at a loss for words, allowing Holtz to continue.

'Here's more: "My thoughts go out to you, my Immortal Beloved, now joyfully, then sadly, waiting to learn whether or not fate will hear us – I can live only wholly with you or not at all."'

'Well, he did live without her, didn't he?' Schindler remarks.

'Did he?' asks Holtz, looking quizzically at the dead man. 'It's a mystery. And why the secret drawer? A guilty liaison with a married woman, perhaps?'

But even before Schindler has time to refute such a claim Holtz catches sight of an exquisite miniature (which must have tumbled from the drawer as it hit the floor) and snatches it up. Then, fearful of the prying eyes of the auctioneer, he retreats to the bedroom to study his trophy in private with the irate Schindler hot on his heels.

'All right, that's enough,' blurts out Schindler after Holtz has been studying the miniature for an age. 'Give it here.'

As he relinquishes it, Holtz poses the question, 'I wonder, is this the Immortal Beloved?'

Schindler scrutinizes the portrait of a striking young woman wearing a turban but displays no sign of recognition. 'Poor craftsmanship, the work of an amateur,' he says dismissively. 'Could be anyone.'

'It's very similar to a portrait I once saw of Therese von Brunswick.'

Unable to make a similar claim, Schindler is piqued. '*If* that should be the case you can rule her out immediately.'

'Why, pray?'

Schindler gives a superior smile. 'She became a nun. I'd say the candidate for your Immortal Beloved was her cousin, Countess Giulietta Guicciardi.'

'On whose authority? Not the Countess herself, surely . . .'

'No, I never met her,' admits Schindler, 'but I heard from the mouth of Beethoven himself that at one time he was madly in love with her. And there *was* cause for secrecy – the obstacle being her father. Now may I kindly see the remaining documents? We've wasted enough time in idle speculation as it is.'

Grateful to his reluctant colleague for providing a clue to a mystery that is beginning to intrigue him, Holtz relinquishes some of the papers with a smile. 'Certainly, old man, you may be right. It could be Giulietta. After all, she did inspire the most romantic music he ever wrote.'

'This is interesting,' enthuses Schindler, ignoring him and reading away. 'Listen to this.'

But Holtz has already turned away from him and is drifting back to the music room, totally absorbed with the yellowing pages, which he handles with the utmost care. He can almost imagine Beethoven himself speaking the words dashed off with passion so many years ago.

> Yes, I am resolved to wander so long away from you until I can fly to your arms and say . . . that I am really at *home* with you, and can . . . send my soul enwrapped in you on to the Lord of Spirits. No one else can ever possess my heart – never, never, oh God, why must one be parted from one whom one so loves . . . And yet my life in Vienna is now a wretched life.

And there, almost within reach, the author of those ardent feelings lies cold and lifeless as Dr Warwuch drills a hole in his bare skull with clinical precision. Holtz's eyes brim with tears as he reads on.

> . . . your love makes me at once the happiest and unhappiest of men – at my age I need a steady quiet life – can that be so in our connection? Be calm, only by a calm consideration of our existence can we achieve our purposes to live together – be calm – love me – today – yesterday – tomorrow – what tearful longings I have for you – my life, my all, farewell . . . Oh continue to love me – never misjudge the most faithful heart of your beloved, ever thine, ever mine, ever ours – Ludwig.

From nowhere a hand appears and snatches the letters from him. Now it is Schindler's turn to make a cold and factual appraisal. Holtz makes no effort to retrieve them. A macabre sound has distracted him. Fascinated, he turns to see the doctor sawing away methodically at Beethoven's skull. Soon he would be examining the Master's brain. Oh, that he could reveal the sight and soul of Giulietta irretrievably lost in those grey, congealing cells.

TWO

Giulietta

MOONLIGHT FILTERING THROUGH elegant windows hints at surroundings of great luxury. In silhouette a pretty teenager is seated at the piano playing music of great serenity, music that seems to be a manifestation of the very atmosphere itself. Naturally, it could only be the 'Moonlight' Sonata. And on the floor at the young lady's feet lies the shadowy figure of none other than the composer himself. Yes, it is Beethoven at the age of thirty, with one ear pressed hard to the carpeted floor and one hand gripping the shapely ankle of Giulietta Guicciardi, with whom he is very much in love. The serene music, soft moonlight and utter tranquillity of the couple conspire to conjure up a scene of strange intimacy that is shattered by the opening of the door and a flood of light.

The intruder is Count Guicciardi, a sombre man in his late forties, cold and aloof. Too well bred to show the displeasure he feels at the sight of his daughter's untidy guest sprawled unashamedly on the floor grasping her ankle, he remains silent. Beethoven lies still, leaving Giulietta to deal with the situation as she continues to play.

'Oh, Father . . . I did not hear your knock.'

Having gently admonished her father, Giulietta plays a few more bars before proffering an explanation. 'Ludwig's music comes from both heaven and earth, Father, which is why he likes to keep an ear to the ground.'

The Count is incensed by Beethoven's arrogance not only in refusing to acknowledge his presence but in retaining his hold on Giulietta's ankle. 'And a finger on the pulse of his public, I see,' he remarks dryly. 'When you are satiated with the food of love, my child, perhaps you and your guest would care to join me in a meal of a more conventional nature.'

Then, as the Count bows and silently closes the door behind him, Beethoven kisses Giulietta's ankle, gets to his feet and sits beside her on the piano stool. The moment of intimacy created by the music has passed.

'What did he say?' asks Beethoven.

'Surely you heard?'

'I heard only the music.'

'Musicians usually stand up when he enters the room. This is a new experience for him.'

'And one he is obviously not yet ready for. I shouldn't have come here.'

A shadow of pique crosses Giulietta's face. She stops playing. 'You had to meet eventually. We can't go on trysting secretly in Vienna for ever. We need his blessing.'

'Do we?'

Giulietta averts a familiar argument by changing the subject. 'Do you habitually listen to music on the floor?'

'It depends on the ankles. You played it well.'

'I did nothing. The music flowed like an electric current. I felt it.'

Beethoven takes the score off the music rest and presents her with it. 'It's yours. I give it to you.'

Giulietta is lost for words. She is overwhelmed by the generosity of his gift. Beethoven kisses her full on the mouth, and she responds ardently.

In a setting rivalling the Hall of Mirrors at Versailles, the remnants of an exquisite meal are being cleared away by an army of servants. Beethoven, a bit drunk, sips brandy and picks his teeth with a candle snuffer. This amuses Giulietta as much as it appals the Count, who for the moment does not betray his true feelings.

'Van Beethoven . . . sounds vaguely aristocratic,' remarks the Count. 'Did your ancestors own land?'

Beethoven's reply verges on the arrogant. 'No, they worked it. They were peasants. Beethoven – beet-basher in Flemish. The van? Alas, Count, not the same as the noble 'von' – as if true nobility can be stamped in the womb! So you see, Count, here you are trying to be civil to a man who is neither "noble" nor – worse – Viennese.'

The Count tries a little sarcasm. 'You would perhaps prefer that we address each other as "comrade".'

Beethoven is unphased. 'Count, you can call me "prole" for all I care, and

I'll reserve the right to call you what I like. Names signify nothing. Beethoven, Bacchus, Bonaparte – ah, there's a combination – music, wine, brotherhood!'

'You laud a name that could bring the world crashing about our ears.'

Beethoven replies with a grin. '*Your* world, not mine.'

Giulietta watches their growing antagonism with delight, and though she deems it prudent to remain silent she obviously takes the side of the radical.

'Think of it – a united Europe; frontiers broken down,' enthuses Beethoven. 'The brotherhood of man! Is there any finer thing on God's earth, eh? Think, Count, what wonders, yet inconceivable, might be seen when a man – any man – celebrated for no other reason than that he *is* a man and not a monkey may be free to express himself, develop, grow, create! Given such liberty, what wonders might a man conceive? It's the new age, Count. I'd like to meet this Bonaparte. He's ambitious, but not just for himself – d'ye see that? He's for glory, but for all people. A self-made man, by God! And no silver nappy pins. You fear this? Why, for God's sake?'

Appalled by the outsider's revolutionary philosophy, the Count remains tight-lipped, which only urges Beethoven on to even wilder flights of fancy.

'Bonaparte marches through Europe with a new world in his hands, and how does Austria greet this new dawn? By wondering if there's going to be a shortage of beer and *sausages*! Well, fill your larder, Count. Our little corporal will be in Vienna within a month.'

'And you, no doubt, will welcome this godless Corsican on your fiddle!' sneers the Count.

'My God, I say, "Aye!"' Fiddle, flute, fife and drum – a new symphony,' declaims Beethoven, rising to his feet in exultation. 'Not for one godless Corsican, Count, but for what he represents to my kind. His country is the world, and his religion is to do good.'

'Many of your fellow countrymen would argue otherwise,' the Count remarks.

'I know,' says Beethoven, sinking back into his chair. 'I've given charity concerts for their widows, their men sacrificed for a putrefying monarch who, like Lazarus, won't lie down.'

Giulietta, who has been a silent but excited observer of this extraordinary scene, summons up the courage to speak. 'A state without the means of some change, Father, is without the means of its conservation.'

'Bravo! Well said!' shouts Beethoven.

'I'm quite familiar with Edmund Burke's pamphleteering, my child,' says the Count condescendingly. 'He reminds us that in France it was not the aristo-crats alone that went to the guillotine but also the parasites that fed upon them.' Beethoven flushes scarlet while the Count, knowing that he has scored a point, follows it up. 'I understand you made the acquaintance of my daughter at Prince Lichnovsky's where you are more or less a permanent house guest.'

'Haven't you heard the news?' retorts Beethoven. 'I've relinquished my quarters at the palace. I couldn't abide the smell . . .' The Count raises an eye-brow as Beethoven continues. 'I've never been able to play the piano and kiss someone's arse at the same time. I live in a tenement now with my nose to the keyboard. I no longer sing for my supper.'

The Count frowns as Giulietta stifles a laugh. 'But what if I requested you to play a bagatelle for us as a little digestif?' he enquires.

'I'd say that my work is not a glass of liver salts. Goodnight, Your Majesty.'

Whereupon Beethoven gets up and walks briskly from the room. Count Guicciardi is outraged, yet there is a kind of understanding between the two men. Giulietta's eyes are full of tears. Why are parents so impossible?

The next morning finds the lovers taking the air in the artfully landscaped grounds of Count Guicciardi's extensive estate. Beethoven, bare-headed with his hair in disarray, is lying on the grass, his eyes avidly following Giulietta as she soars above him on a garlanded swing. Their mood is carefree and mildly flirtatious.

'A little digestif!' he mutters scornfully. 'If he suffers from flatulence he needs an enema, not music.'

'Almost as bad as people who treat music like wallpaper, as a background to conversation.'

'Well said. If I had to choose between a man and music, I'd say give me music any day.'

Suddenly Giulietta's dainty slipper flies off her foot. Beethoven catches it in mid-flight. He jumps up and starts bellowing a melody while conducting an imaginary orchestra with the slipper.

'How do you like my new cantata?'

'The orchestra's in fine form,' enthuses Giulietta, 'but the chorus isn't quite together.'

'Chorus?'

From her vantage point on the swing Giulietta nods towards a herd of grazing sheep. Beethoven follows her gaze and laughs. 'Yes, they are a little woolly.'

'But our feathered soloist is in great voice. Why is she so popular with you composers?'

He listens for the soloist in vain, and fearful of revealing the secret of his growing deafness he resorts to bluff. 'All birds sound the same to me. I can't tell a wren from a rooster.'

Giulietta cannot take him seriously and laughs.

This disconcerts him and pushes him deeper into trouble as the bird sings on. 'If you're talking of popularity, it must be a nightingale . . .'

She begins to suspect something is amiss and checks her carefree swinging.

Beethoven catches her look and realizes he has guessed wrong. '. . . Except it's broad daylight,' he adds.

Giulietta is stationary now and overcome with confusion, while he is becoming desperate. 'There's a harpsichord piece by Rameau called "The Hen".' He looks into her eyes for a clue but sees only disbelief. 'But even I can recognize a chicken. How about a mistle thrush?' he chances. There is silence for a moment, broken by the incessant notes of the bird. 'A *late* mistle thrush?' he hazards.

Giulietta is completely at a loss and remains silent.

'Then it must be a mockingbird. No? Obviously not!' So in desperation he adopts the cry of a fairground barker. "Ard luck, mister, there's your four tries gawn!'

Tears of pity fill Giulietta's eyes, but they only enrage the desperate man. 'Then tell me! For God's sake.'

She is trembling now and crying. He grabs her by the shoulders, shakes her violently and shouts, 'Say something, damn you!'

She is now sobbing uncontrollably. Beethoven becomes increasingly violent, almost demented.

'Speak, you bitch, speak!' He slaps her hard across the face and then stands back, appalled by his action.

At the same time the shock frees Giulietta's tongue. 'A cuckoo! It's a cuckoo!' she shouts and starts crying hysterically.

Beethoven, a lost and broken man, simply mutters. 'Of course. Daquin, Haydn . . . I should have guessed.'

Giulietta, realizing the depth of his misery, overcomes her own distress.

Still sobbing, she throws her arms around Beethoven and hugs him tight as the inane call of the cuckoo resounds through the trees, endlessly mocking.

Hand in hand, Beethoven and Giulietta walk up the drive flanked by statues and formal gardens towards the mansion. The composer, now his secret is shared, looks pale but somewhat relieved, but the young Countess is emotionally drained.

'I don't know what to say.'

'Say nothing. I'm aware that urchins follow me in the streets. That I talk to myself. If they knew I couldn't hear either, it would be intolerable.'

'You've seen doctors, of course.'

'The last one nearly drowned me in a tonic bath. Gave me diarrhoea. The one before that poured nut oil and tea in my ear. I was delirious for a week.'

'Exactly what do you experience?'

'My ears buzz and hum all night.'

'Can you hear some things?'

'It comes and goes. I'm guessing for the most part, or lip-reading. If I go to the theatre I sit right at the front. At any distance I can't hear the voices – what's worse, the instruments.'

'But you can catch what I'm saying now?'

'Oh, I can hear you – slightly. Surprisingly, many people don't notice my . . . my . . . Perhaps I'm absent-minded. They attribute it to that. Besides the doctors and yourself, nobody suspects.'

Giulietta raises her voice. 'But your music . . .'

'Don't shout at me. It's unbearable. I still have some hearing.' Beethoven checks himself and calms down. 'It will be several years before I am completely deaf. As for music, I can hear it all the time in my head.' He smiles and takes her hand. 'Or through my thick skull,' he taps his head with her hand. 'Vibrations, as if my head were a bell.'

Giulietta becomes excited. 'Then I'd be your clapper; your contact with the world. Between us we'd sound a carillon that would shake the heavens.' She gives him a playful hammering on the head. 'Ding-dong, ding-dong, went the great bell of Bonn.'

Laughing, Beethoven ducks, dodges and defends himself. 'Easy, easy, don't strike too hard. Nothing sounds worse than a cracked bell.' She laughingly complies, allowing him to strike a deeper note. 'Some bells resound to a breeze, a whisper, an echo . . . even silence.'

Giulietta instinctively feels he is right, that she may not be the one and only answer to his life but determines not to let him realize this. '*Your* breeze comes from a great void, my love. *I* could be much more than that.'

'Ah – but what would become of you when you had grown to fear me!' He pulls a hideous face like a zombie, causing her to squeal with half-frightened laughter like a child and run off into the house. Beethoven follows slowly, his countenance a mixture of anguish, pain and gentleness. But there is resolve there, too.

It is night in the music room, and Giulietta, sitting at the piano in despair, is doing her best to repair the damage. Her father the Count, deeply concerned over his daughter's welfare, stands immobile before the fire, which provides the sole illumination.

'It was *not* arrogance, Father. It was the only way he could *hear* the music – through the vibrations from the floor.'

'And is this unfortunate man aware of the fact that you wish to marry him?'

'I was going to broach the subject today, but in the circumstances it would have seemed like pity.'

'And has he declared himself to you?'

'Out of deference to our social position, no. I feel he is waiting for me to make the first move.'

'Then there's no harm done. He is without rank, fortune or permanent engagement. As a performer his days are numbered and, as they dwindle, so will his income. Unable to support you, he'd be reduced to an embittered cripple begging your charity.'

'He is too proud for that, Father, too noble. And whatever I had I would give him freely.'

'Which is why he would hate you for it.'

'But I love him, Father.'

'Then you have no alternative but to send him away,' concludes the Count, moving towards his distraught child. Then kissing her tenderly on the forehead he begins to take his leave, secretly thankful his victory has so easily been achieved.

As he closes the door Giulietta begins to cry.

THREE

A Fresh Suspect

BACK IN BEETHOVEN's lodgings Holtz continues to study the love letters and ruminate over the identity of the Immortal Beloved. Behind him, through the doorway, in the next room Dr Warwuch is seen performing the autopsy, watched by Danhauser the mask-maker and his assistant Tantfl.

'I can't believe these letters were written to Giulietta,' mutters Holtz. 'My guess is they were addressed to a more mature woman – not necessarily in years, mind you. And if there was a barrier between them, I'm not convinced it was an intolerant parent; more like a cuckolded husband.'

Schindler, engrossed in his own papers, answers curtly, 'Beethoven was a man of honour.'

Holtz ignores him. 'And Giulietta did marry – a year after she and Beethoven parted.'

'Count Gallenberg, a second-rate composer,' says Schindler dismissively.

'But rich,' declares Holtz with authority. 'They left for Naples directly after the ceremony; seems they couldn't get out of Beethoven's reach quick enough – and as far as I'm aware Naples is where they remain to this day.'

Schindler is a little ruffled at such erudition, but for the moment he is more excited about his own discovery, which, in the interest of one-upmanship, he can contain no longer.

'Love pales to insignificance beside the emotions expressed in this document, my friend. The writing is almost indecipherable, but it appears to be a suicide note precipitated by the terrible realization that for the rest of his life he was condemned to increasing and total deafness. It's a veritable cry of despair to God.'

Holtz takes the paper from him before he can object.

'Let me ... Ah, lucky for you, this one is dated – 10 October 1802 – just after he's left Giulietta.' A sudden inspiration strikes him. 'Perhaps the shadow between Beethoven and his beloved was not human but divine; which wouldn't rule out Therese at all. And this portrait – it's just as Beethoven once described her.'

Schindler, who was never taken into the composer's confidence to a similar extent, simply ignores him.

FOUR

Therese

STANDING IN THE doorway of Beethoven's music room is Therese
von Brunswick, a strikingly handsome woman in her mid-twenties,
dressed in the Greek style then fashionable, and which fits her picture
of herself as Priestess of the Truth to perfection. Across the room Beethoven
sits at his desk covering a sheet of manuscript with a busy scrawl. His head is
haloed in bright sunlight, and this, combined with the simple robe he is wearing
and the austere surroundings, gives the impression more of a monk at work
than a composer. Therese senses something of this, but it does not stop her
breaking the spell.

'Luigi.' Beethoven does not hear, so she tries again, considerably louder.
'Luigi.'

Still no response, so she crosses the room and boldly taps him on the
shoulder. Beethoven spins around angrily.

'Never do that again! Never!' he shouts. 'Do you hear?'

Therese flinches slightly but manages a smile.

Beethoven is unforgiving. 'Announce yourself like any other pupil. All
lessons today are cancelled.'

Therese refrains from stating the obvious and apologizes. 'I'm sorry. I was
eager to give you this present.'

Beethoven remains unrelenting until he sees the painting Therese takes from
a protective folder – a vivid watercolour of an eagle flying into the sun. The artist
cannot hide her excitement as a flicker of pleasure crosses Beethoven's face.

'Turn it over.'

Beethoven does so and reads the inscription aloud: 'To that rare genius,
the great artist, the good human being – from TB.' He examines the painting
once more and, impressed with Therese's symbolic portrayal of him, starts

to thaw. 'So that's how you imagine me,' he mutters gruffly. 'I'm flattered.'

'I saw your ballet before I really knew you.'

'*Prometheus?*'

'Yes, man in the guise of an eagle stealing a little heavenly fire to warm the hearts of us poor mortals with its magic.'

'And punished for his trouble,' adds Beethoven.

'The gods forgave him in the end.'

'They were Greek gods. They're dead,' scoffs Beethoven. 'And I'm still half deaf. Sometimes I curse the God that made me, put this . . . enigma inside me. Sometimes I wish I was living the life of a peasant, bringing in the harvest.'

'Perhaps that is our answer – the simple life,' she suggests.

'Prickly heat and blisters wouldn't suit you,' replies Beethoven with a grin, 'and I only said "sometimes". I don't subscribe to the cult of the noble savage. I've been there.'

'Then you must learn to be resigned to your fate,' she says primly.

'Resignation! What a wretched thought. Is that all that's left for me? If I thought fate was going to deny me just one day of pure joy . . . No, that would be too hard. My God!'

His manuscript is beginning to smoulder. The bottle glass in one of the window-panes is acting like a magnifying glass for the rays of the sun. Suddenly the paper catches alight. He grabs a bottle of wine and quenches the flames. At the same time his pessimism goes up in smoke.

'Here, dear, have a drink. We'll both set Vienna alight. All in good time.'

'You've still got the divine fire,' laughs Therese.

'Oh dear, your witticisms are almost as bad as mine,' Beethoven says, giving her a friendly peck on the cheek.

'It's good to see you laughing again.' Therese is glad to be back in his good books. 'Come down to Martonvásár for the weekend. You need a holiday, and Mama is away.'

'I haven't been to the country for weeks,' he says with a sigh.

'There's nothing to fear, my love.'

'Not if one's an eagle,' he says ruminatively.

'Well, Master, do I get my lesson now?'

'Better lock the door then.'

'I already have.'

Beethoven laughs. They embrace. The lesson commences.

FIVE

Prometheus

O N   T H E   B R U N S W I C K   estate in the region of Martonvásár in Hungary an open-air ballet is in progress. A small orchestra nestles to one side of a Watteau-like glade, the trees of which form a natural proscenium for an entertainment designed for an audience of one, Ludwig van Beethoven, enthroned on a capacious gilt chair attended by flunkeys serving food and drink. As the overture comes to an end Therese appears to announce the programme. She looks more Grecian than ever.

'Greetings, dear honoured guest. It gives me great pleasure to announce *The Creatures of Prometheus*, a ballet in three acts with music by Luigi van Beethoven...' The composer bows and gives a little smile, encouraging Therese to continue. '... freely adapted from the original scenario of Salvatore Viganò by Therese von Brunswick and performed by her family and friends ... and servants.' She curtsies rather self-consciously to Beethoven, whose smile of expectation gives way to a look of apprehension as Therese chatters on. 'Act I, in which the artist Prometheus, disguised as an eagle, steals sacred fire from the Gods.'

A nervous glance at Beethoven, and she has disappeared behind a bush. As the band strikes up again her brother Franz, dressed as an eagle, wings his way towards the sun – an illuminated orb shining from the depths of the glade. The eagle flies between pirouetting planets, danced by girls holding lanterns, past a streaking comet in the form of a leaping dancer with a silver scarf, through a group of servants holding a galaxy of candelabra representing stars and up a camouflaged ramp to the sun. With a twist of its mighty beak the eagle wrenches off a gleaming fragment and dives into a billowing white cloud of smoke that is immediately suffused with a brilliant golden glow.

The music stops and the delighted Beethoven applauds. With a smile of pleasure Therese appears from behind her bush, for a further announcement.

'Act II, in which Prometheus, aided by the heavenly embers, gives his creations life.'

As the band strikes up once more Therese is joined by her pretty sister, Josephine, her junior by a few years. As still as two Greek statues the girls wait patiently while Franz slips out of his eagle costume into that of an artist closely resembling Beethoven, a fact that does not go unrecognized by the composer. Prometheus the man scatters glowing dust on his sculptures and gives them life. His creatures dance, first with each other, then with their creator to whom they sing a magical vocalise.

The girls themselves, beautiful, sylph-like, attired in gauze dresses and transparent dragonfly wings, conjure up an effect both magical and erotic. Beethoven is completely seduced until a sudden thunderbolt flashes from the sky, striking Prometheus deaf! The band still plays, the girls still sing – apparently – but not a sound is heard by either Prometheus or the composer, who is trembling with emotion.

Prometheus draws a dagger to kill himself but is persuaded by his creations to stay his hand. Sobbing, he falls to the ground in despair.

The 'silent' band stops playing. Therese glances at her brother and sister, who are clearly afraid that things have gone too far. Not so. She summons up the courage to see things through. Solemnly she announces the next act – presumably so, for though her lips move no sound issues from her mouth. Beethoven, shaken to the core, only partially succeeds in hiding his distress.

The third act commences in a terrible silence broken only by the sound of Beethoven's own heartbeat.

The band plays an inaudible accompaniment to the silent song of the sisters as they lead Prometheus towards a crucifix, which appears silhouetted before the setting sun. On his knees Prometheus prays for forgiveness, and as his prayer is answered the glade suddenly echoes with a twittering cacophony as the musicians blow on a variety of whistles, producing a riot of raucous birdsong. Beethoven reacts to this badly. Obviously cousin Giulietta has been talking.

Only when the musicians revert to their regular instruments and strike up the joyous music to the Finale of the ballet is Beethoven able to control his distress a little. Shepherds and shepherdesses join the sisters and Prometheus in a dance of thanksgiving. The final triumphant chords drift through the trees. The company turn to the composer and make their bows.

Beethoven's head is buried in his hands. He appears to be sobbing in despair. With a wave of her hand Therese dismisses the company and in some alarm runs up to him and rests her hands on his shoulder. When he throws his head back there are tears running down his face and he is shaking with laughter; but the effort shows and Therese is not fooled by his play-acting.

'Oh dear,' exclaims Beethoven. 'If only I'd known what I let myself in for when I accepted that commission. I never dreamed I'd end up as a Greek myth. In our version Prometheus was a sculptor who was blinded not –'

'Prometheus was a great artist, and so are you,' interrupts Therese. 'And you both stole inspiration from the gods. You both suffered the thunderbolt of divine wrath. You both got burned.'

'*Stole?*' exclaims Beethoven. 'You really see God as the great avenger, don't you? You see me as a *thief?* Are you *that* stupid, woman?'

Therese loves Beethoven, but she loves the truth more and is determined to make Beethoven face the truth as she sees it. 'However you acquired it, you have something unique among mortal men. It's only fitting you should be called upon to sacrifice something for the privilege.'

'Privilege!' Beethoven is outraged. 'So we're back to *that*, are we? "Little man, do not dare to enquire, or you'll be punished for your presumption!" That's your mystery? For that I must lose my most treasured faculty?'

'Not necessarily,' replies Therese calmly. 'Prometheus redeemed his faculties by praying to God.'

'Ah, but dare I ask which god, Therese? Perhaps this eagle wants to fly higher than *your* heaven – perhaps he wants to see what lies beyond.'

She takes his hand and leads him towards the glade and – she hopes – eternal enlightenment. 'You said yourself the Greek gods are dead. Christ is risen from the dead. Seek salvation through prayer to Jesus. A miracle brought forth your music. A miracle may yet restore your hearing, if you have faith.'

They have arrived at a life-sized crucifix. Still holding his hand, Therese kneels before it and looks at him beseechingly. 'Will you join me in prayer?'

Beethoven hesitates for a moment, then drops her hand. Therese looks sorrowful. The sky begins to darken, heralding an approaching storm.

'When I choose to speak to the gods it's in their own tongue,' he replies solemnly.

Therese ignores him and bends her head in prayer as Beethoven sits down at the piano abandoned by one of the musicians and starts to play. At first the music is meditative, every note a complete prayer in itself, even when the growing thunder forces him to play louder.

But, gradually, the prayer becomes protest against the gods, who seem determined to drown the music of the mortal who has dared to challenge their glory. Therese, who has ceased praying, realizes this and watches fearfully for the outcome of the battle. Beethoven's playing becomes demonic. The darkening glade is illuminated by flashes of lightning. He is nearly demented as he roars above his own efforts to storm the angry heavens.

'Did I rob you? Did I take too much? I thought it was a gift. Of course I took it! So you punish me and mock me with your thunder to remind me I'm not totally deaf – not yet. Well, finish me off. Prometheus defies you: destroy him! He stole your fire: let him perish by fire. I defy you! Me! I dare! . . . Well, come on! Is it Zeus? Jehovah? Three in one? Make me whole or kill me. Show me your power. Kill me or show me!' And he raises his fist against the sky like a lightning conductor while pounding out massive chords with his free hand. 'Destroy me, damn you. Destroy me.'

For an answer the mocking gods send not fire but water. It begins to rain – torrentially. Beethoven plays a few ineffectual watery chords, then catches Therese's eye, which flashes with a strange gleam of triumph. He has mocked God, and he has been punished yet again for his arrogance.

'But for Christ's sake do not . . . laugh at me.'

Blind with misery, Beethoven slams down the piano lid and staggers off into the wood.

Back in Beethoven's lodgings Schindler continues to read from the revealing documents:

From year to year my hopes of being cured have gradually been shattered and finally I have been forced to accept the prospect of a permanent infirmity. I was in despair and on the point of putting an end to my life . . . The only thing that held me back was my art. For indeed it seemed impossible to leave the world before I had produced all the works that I felt the urge to compose and thus I have dragged on this miserable existence . . . a truly miserable existence. Patience – that is the virtue, I am told, which I must now choose for my guide, and I now possess it. Perhaps my condition will improve, perhaps not; at any rate I am resigned.

Holtz, who has been hanging on every word, has had enough. 'Patience, indeed. There sounds the voice of St Therese the virtuous. Beethoven may have flirted with her, but I doubt if he would have stood her preaching for long. He was too free a spirit. What else does he say?'

Schindler scans another page. 'He instructs his brother to perform certain duties on his death and divide his property equally between himself and Beethoven's idiotic nephew, so I'm not surprised he locked this up.'

'Because he changed his mind and left everything to the idiot?' suggests Holtz.

'Exactly. Then why preserve this one?'

'He preserved it because he had to express his distress in writing. Because there was no one to whom he could bare his soul, not even the Immortal Beloved.'

'Holtz, this Immortal Beloved is becoming an obsession with you. You've eliminated Guicciardi and her cousin Therese. Who's next? Why not keep it in the family and say Josephine?'

'I was just going to mention Josephine,' admits Holtz.

'I hardly think he'd play court to both sisters at the same time!'

'I never said he did, but when he realized Therese was destined for the cloisters he may have turned his attention elsewhere, and with Josephine he wouldn't have had far to look. He often spoke of her with great affection.'

Schindler reluctantly agrees. 'They were both pupils of his, I grant you, and he only instructed those he smiled upon, it's true.'

Holtz is lost in thought. Schindler follows his gaze to the next room where Dr Warwuch has completed his autopsy and is washing his hands while Danhauser and Tantfl are covering the dead composer's head in plaster.

SIX

Fallen Idol

A N IMPATIENT RAP sounds on Beethoven's door, which is flung
open to reveal a breathless Therese carrying a newspaper. She
enters briskly and locks the door behind her.

I'm here, Luigi,' she shouts, taking off her hat and flinging it on the chair.
'I'm here for my lesson, but first I must give you the news . . .' She notices the
curtains of the four-poster bed are drawn. Giggles and whispers sound from
within, rendering her speechless, then startled, as Beethoven's voice thunders
through the drapes.

'The news can wait. Seat yourself at the piano and we'll start the lesson.'

Therese is so nonplussed that she involuntarily obeys.

'Today we will extemporize,' declaims the voice of the Master, as with a
tremendous effort Therese regains some of her composure.

'I'm afraid I'm very late. I shall take my leave. Next week I shall be
punctual.'

More whispers issue from the bed as Therese leaves her newspaper on the
piano and makes for the door.

'If you disobey you need never come back,' warns the voice of authority.

Therese pauses, then sits at the piano and nervously clears her throat.
'Ready, Master.'

'You will extemporize on a theme of love – *molto amoroso*,' comes the
stern command.

Therese's inclination is to jump to her feet and run to the door, but pride
overcomes distress and compels her to accept Beethoven's challenge. As
sounds of love-making issue from behind the curtains, Therese improvises a
concerto for piano and four-poster complete with grunts, groans, squeaks,
bumps and occasional commands from the conductor.

'*Accelerando . . . apassionata . . . fff . . . tranquillo, pianissimo . . .*' and eventually '*finito*'.

Therese suffers considerable torment during this performance, and only her determination not to give way to what she considers to be 'weakness of character' enables her to echo every nuance of the lovers with great finesse until she gradually masters her feelings. Determined to show she is unphased she manages to imbue her playing with a touch of parody by the time she reaches the Finale. Her inner turmoil is certainly not evident to the couple behind the curtains who have only the evidence of their ears.

'Bravo!' shouts Beethoven with genuine enthusiasm. 'A touch heavy on the *apassionata*, and I detected a note of *con parodia* in the Finale, but for all that a highly commendable performance. Next week we'll play a duet together.'

Feminine laughter from within the confines of the four-poster followed by whispers to the Master and his explosive mirth all combine to send Therese off in such a hurry that she forgets her hat lying on the chair. However, she manages a spirited parting shot while unlocking the door. 'Next week you can play with yourself, Master.'

More snuffled laughter follows as Therese slams the door behind her. The curtains of the four-poster stir, then part, revealing the flushed face of her sister Josephine.

'She's gone to confession, I shouldn't wonder.'

Slipping out of bed, swathed in a sheet, she relocks the door.

Beethoven, in a dressing-gown, rolls over and sits on the side of the bed, looks about the room and sighs. 'Oh dear, I was too hard on her.'

'She enjoyed it as much as we did. I know her,' says Josephine, smirking. 'My dear sister positively revels in pain – it makes her feel indescribably holy. Believe me, you've given her existence a justification at last. She will dutifully pray for you for the rest of her life.'

'In that case a good time was had by all,' says Beethoven, licking his lips. 'My, but I've worked up a thirst.'

'I'll get you a drink, precious,' says Josephine, kissing him on the cheek. 'Wine?'

'What else?' he replies, giving her a playful slap on the bum as she hops out of bed having spied a bottle on the piano. As she pours a glass she catches sight of her sister's message scrawled on the newspaper. Alarmed at what she reads she attempts to hide it beneath a manuscript but is observed by Beethoven's eagle eye.

'What are you hiding? Did she leave me a *billet-doux*?' He grabs the newspaper, from which he reads aloud, with disbelief, 'Napoleon Crowns Himself Emperor.'

'And what do you make of my sister's comment that "we must put an end to such idolatry"?'

Beethoven can barely comprehend that his hero has feet of clay and answers in his own way, taking his time. 'Napoleon crowns himself Emperor. So! He, too, is nothing but an ordinary creature. He, too, will trample underfoot all the rights of man. Indulge his ambition! Exalt himself above all others!' He snatches up a thick stack of manuscript and waves it angrily in the air. 'Look! My "heroic" symphony. I have written a symphony glorifying a tyrant! Look, our names share the title page side by side. Even with that bastard I made a mistake!'

Beethoven pushes it in front of Josephine's face then swiftly crosses to the stove, removes the lid and looks down into the flames.

Josephine grabs him firmly by the arm. 'What are you doing? You can't – please! Don't destroy it – it's part of you.'

'That's very intuitive of you!' he replies, momentarily caught off balance. Made even angrier by her insight and his own vulnerability, he pushes her hard and sends her sprawling to the floor and prepares to consign the score to the flames.

'No, don't. Please, no!' pleads Josephine.

Beethoven hesitates, trembling with anger. 'From now on I'll make no explanations for my music. You can all guess what the hell I'm up to!'

Then with a gesture of contempt he rips off the page of dedication and throws it into the fire. Taking a pencil, he scrawls across the title page of the manuscript a new dedication, which he reads aloud, 'To the memory of a great man.'

Overcome with relief, Josephine takes his hand, kisses it and presses it against her cheek.

SEVEN

Mistaken Identity

*I*T IS NIGHT in a back street in Vienna. An effigy of Napoleon complete with cocked hat hangs in flames from a lamp-post. The poor of the city watch him burn. Beethoven and Josephine, clutching bottles of wine from which they occasionally drink, observe from the shadows. A tear trickles down Beethoven's cheek while throbbing in his mind resounds the poignant strains of the great funeral march from the 'Eroica' Symphony.

Out of the mists a strange procession painfully drags its way. Are they prisoners, infirm refugees or soldiers maimed in battle? And those bundles the women hug to their breasts – are they salvaged clothes or dead children? Those objects they push so laboriously – are they broken guns or carts loaded with shabby possessions? Those tattered shreds they drag through the mud – were they once proud banners carried on high, promising brotherhood, liberty and joy? The people's eyes search for an answer as they shuffle endlessly onward. How long have they suffered their tribulations? How long will they continue to suffer? Where is he who has promised them all and given them nothing? Their saviour has many faces; one of them – a man of straw – hangs burning on a lamp-post. He lights their forlorn faces with a bloody glow. Out of the mist they come and into the mist they go. Beethoven's music laments their passing. They are the real heroes of his symphony, as he will eventually come to realize. As the procession disappears two militiamen arrive on the scene shouting and causing a commotion.

With the exception of Beethoven and Josephine, who draw closer to the burning tyrant, the little crowd melts rapidly into the night. With their pikes the militiamen pull down the effigy into the street where Napoleon's smouldering hat bounces at Beethoven's feet. Scooping it up he hastily dips it into a horse trough and puts it on his head. Then, sticking his hand in his frock coat, he struts up and down amid the flames, looking for all the world like his fallen hero.

Despite the protests of Josephine, Beethoven is arrested by the militiamen, who consider him either drunk or mad or both and drag him off into the darkness swigging from his bottle.

In the local lock-up a gaoler is incarcerating Beethoven.

'I am not Napoleon,' he shouts. 'I am Beethoven.'

'And I am Jesus of Nazareth,' replies the blasé gaoler.

Suddenly an angry bearded face appears looking over Beethoven's shoulder. It is another deluded offender.

'Blasphemers. I *am* Jesus of Nazareth.'

Amused, Beethoven plays along. 'Please forgive me, Your Holiness. I say, you couldn't rustle up a small miracle for me, could you?'

'Sometimes I wonder if I'm running a lock-up or a loony-bin,' remarks the long-suffering gaoler as he makes off down the corridor leaving Beethoven alone in his cell with Jesus.

'Who are you?' demands Jesus. 'He who comes riding the dark horse or he who comes singing Hosannas to God's glory?'

'Try Barabbas,' replies Beethoven with a wry grin.

'God will help you, my son.'

'Oh man – help thyself,' declaims Beethoven.

The Saviour is shocked. 'You would exalt yourself above God!'

'What did you say?' asks Beethoven, hard of hearing.

'You would exalt yourself above God,' the Saviour shouts.

'I'm all for sharing that divine joy we've heard so much about,' Beethoven affirms. 'That's what I'm after.'

'In the fullness of time, my son. Meanwhile you must bow to your fate.'

Beethoven freaks out, hammers on the cell door, crying out in protest, 'I shall seize Fate by the throat. It shall not crush me!'

Suddenly voices are heard. They belong to Josephine and the gaoler, who is fumbling with his keys while muttering an apology. ''Ow did I know he was Beethoven? He don't look like Beethoven – no more than 'im in there ain't no Jesus.'

'Hurry, Gaoler, quickly,' urges Josephine.

'Steady on, Josephine. I don't think he's the gaoler at all. Too nervous, too humble,' jokes Beethoven.

Finally the door is open. Beethoven steps out of the cell and glances behind him at the pathetic figure of the Saviour.

'Wait. Can't we resurrect Jesus from the tomb while we're at it?'

'I can't, Your Honour,' laments the gaoler. 'He's in for breaking and entering – the palace. Found in the Emperor's bedroom at midnight trying to give him thirty pieces of silver.'

'For selling out to tyranny, I presume,' says Beethoven. 'Well done. Goodnight, Jesus. Honour thy father!'

As the little group makes its way down the corridor Josephine explains, 'I went straight to the Lord Mayor. He was most upset and sends his personal apologies – also the state coach.'

But this is lost on Beethoven, who is singing 'O come all ye faithful'.

In the street outside, Beethoven, still tipsy, is assisted into the coach by Josephine and the gaoler, who closes the door behind them, cap in hand. As the coach drives off the composer shouts a passing thought to him. 'You were wrong about me. You could be wrong about Jesus.'

As the exhortations of the Saviour escape through the cell window and fall upon the ears of the gaoler, it is clear that Beethoven has sown a seed of doubt.

EIGHT

The Dummy

*A*FEW STREETS AWAY and a few minutes later a dozing night watchman blinks awake as the Lord Mayor's coach clatters over the cobblestones and screeches to a halt outside the Gallerie Müller, the impressive building that houses Vienna's largest private collection of waxworks. By the time Josephine has helped Beethoven down, the night watchman has lit a lantern and bowed her welcome.

As the coach pulls away, Beethoven, sleepy and still under the influence, takes in his surroundings. 'This isn't my place. Where are we?'

'Tonight we'll spend under my roof,' says Josephine. Your lodgings are full of phantoms.'

Beethoven grunts a non-committal reply.

'Shall I light your way, my lady?' asks the night watchman with a bow.

'No, you may retire.'

'Thank you, my lady.'

Taking the lantern, Josephine leads Beethoven through the door, leaving the night watchman to lock up.

'I thought you said there were no phantoms here,' says a startled Beethoven, suddenly face to face with Bonaparte, mocking, triumphant and macabre in the light of the flickering lantern.

And as Beethoven stares at his fallen hero Josephine endeavours to raise his spirits. 'All genius is ahead of its time. Don't be disheartened. Your music tells of a hero, and one day he will come. The mantle will fit and the sword will be drawn from the stone. The people will rejoice. In the meantime they can sense his spirit in your music.'

Beethoven stares into the eyes of the wax dummy, searching for an answer to the enigma of artistic creation. When he speaks, it is as if to himself.

'There's a funeral march in my symphony. Even as I was composing it I wondered why. Why was I compelled to sound a note of lamentation? I was celebrating liberation, freedom and equality. Why not a joyous march of triumph then, eh? Tonight I found the answer.' He looks questioningly at Josephine, who echoes his thoughts.

'The world must know suffering before it can appreciate joy. Your music is prophetic.'

'Oh ho! We're paying the piper again. Well, my symphony ends on a joyous note, so I'll drink to that.'

'Come, we'll break open a bottle of your favourite wine!' says Josephine brightly.

But they have barely moved two paces before Beethoven stops again. He is looking at two waxworks who in turn stare back at him. One is Haydn, clutching a violin, the other Mozart with a cello. They are both seated near a piano and a vacant stool.

'I thought they were your friends,' says Josephine. 'In any case, their censure is a small price to pay for the lavish accommodation that goes with this display – the largest in Central Europe, and now it's mine. Soon it could be ours.'

The place unnerves Beethoven. He looks around furtively. 'Where's the founder? I don't see him on display.'

But Josephine won't be sidetracked. 'My dear departed husband chose to play the dummy in life. Is it true that you refused to write "pupil of Haydn" on your work when he was your teacher?'

Beethoven puts his arm around the shoulders of the more elderly looking of the two effigies and smiles at him with real affection. 'I refused, yes. The only good thing he ever taught me was generosity. I'd have starved if it had not been for him. He was good to Mozart as well. God rest his soul.' Beethoven lovingly adjusts the wig of the younger effigy and continues to reminisce. 'I'll never forget my first meeting with Papa Haydn. We'd barely exchanged the time of day when he dubbed me "upstart". "You are neither a Goethe nor a Handel, young man. Such souls are no longer born." I'd arrived from Bonn with a letter of introduction from the Elector.'

'Were you not his Chapel Master?' asks Josephine.

'Ha! There was only one Master in his chapel! I was the musical flunkey – livery and all. "A tune for the chapel!" he says, snapping his fingers. "A tune for the closet!" and he snaps them again. Whether he was praying or "performing"

I provided background accompaniment. Nothing too original, you understand; nothing so intrusive as to disturb the flow of undiluted trivia emanating from the dining-table – or from any other place. The commode was in the corner.' He gives Josephine a sly smile, fully aware that he is shocking her. 'My father sang himself hoarse in his service, and when he could no longer sing he tried to drink and whore himself into oblivion. Do you see some irony there, Papa Haydn? Dumb the father, deaf the son. My inheritance – silence. Oh, His Excellency was succinct on the subject of my work: "It's too abrasive!" A-ha, but how to shake off this blowfly, draw his sting? So he packed me off to Vienna, and no doubt posterity will celebrate him as Beethoven's first mentor. I'd applaud his foresight if I did not suspect His Excellency merely chose Haydn because he could spell the old man's name!'

Throughout the ensuing dialogue Beethoven speaks in shrill, piping tones when imitating Haydn and his natural voice when replying, while Mozart watches in frozen amusement. The flickering lantern practically animates them into life. It's almost like a play conceived for a privileged audience of one.

HAYDN: The Elector writes that you wish to follow in our footsteps, to become a symphonist like Mozart and myself.

BEETHOVEN: With respect, I am looking for untrodden snows.

HAYDN: How old are you?

BEETHOVEN: I'm not sure.

HAYDN: Didn't your parents teach you to count?

BEETHOVEN: Yes, but they could never agree.

HAYDN: Past tense?

BEETHOVEN: They're dead. My father died just before Christmas. He was singing his heart out . . .

HAYDN: Hymns?

BEETHOVEN: Boozy ballads, most likely. I wasn't there.

HAYDN: Do you know how many symphonies Mozart had written by the time he died?

BEETHOVEN: More than me, and fewer than you?

HAYDN: He was composing symphonies at the age of eight. By his untimely death at thirty-four he had completed forty-one. Do you know how many I have composed, sir?

BEETHOVEN: Were you his equal, I'd say eighty-two – seeing you must be double his age, Herr Haydn.

HAYDN: You are nothing if not frank, young man. I have written one hundred and four.

BEETHOVEN: Then you are more than his equal if by simple mathematics we could define quality.

HAYDN: And your sum thus far, young man? How many symphonies have you composed to date?

BEETHOVEN: None, sir!

HAYDN: No. And what does that make you, sir?

BEETHOVEN: Unique, Herr Haydn.

Josephine, laughing, asks, 'And Mozart – did you meet him?'

'Once. I was seventeen or so.'

'And?'

Clearly this is a treasured memory not to be shared. He stares at Mozart.

'He had one thing in common with Haydn: an ill-chosen wife. She was like a helpless moth around a flame. Little wonder he ended in a pauper's grave.'

Touched by this revealing performance, Josephine is forced to speak out. 'I'll watch over you. You'll have no fear of penury.'

Beethoven is worried by her materialism. He taps Mozart's forehead. 'Just remember – you have captured only the substance there, not the spirit.'

As Beethoven starts to move off he inadvertently treads on a hidden switch in the floor, which sets the two musical dummies in motion. Haydn stabs away at his violin while Mozart saws away on the cello. The scene is made even more grotesque by a clanging piano, which appears to be played by a ghost. (In actuality it was one of the very first mechanical pianos.) Beethoven is both startled and appalled by this macabre concert, while Josephine is merely annoyed.

'Oh dear, you've spoiled my surprise! It was for your birthday.'

Then to her complete astonishment Beethoven adopts the puppet-like movements of his mechanical colleagues. Seated at the piano, he mimes playing at the keyboard. Josephine claps her hands with delight.

'Perfect! Perfect! You guessed! Why, it's better than the real thing. Oh, if only you would do that for the grand unveiling! Imagine! Everyone would say,

"What a lifelike dummy." And when it was over you'd stand up and take a bow! Priceless. Oh, Ludi, do say you'll do it.'

At this moment the music ends, and Mozart and Haydn jerk into immobility. Not so Beethoven, who lurches to his feet and gives a jerky bow, followed by another and another. Josephine applauds joyfully.

'Bravo! Bravo! All Vienna will flock to see you. You will be my prize exhibit. What a shock they'll get when you spring to life, and arm in arm we walk away in triumph. Oh, how the tongues will wag!'

Josephine extends her arm for Beethoven to take, but he simply continues bowing like an automaton, a fixed imbecilic grin on his face. The joke has gone on too long. Josephine wishes it to end so she shakes Beethoven, even slaps his face, but still the smiling dummy continues to bow. He is still bowing when she runs screaming from the room.

'Therese was right – you are mad! Mad! Mad! Mad!'

And that was her last memory of her mad lost love – a grinning, bowing dummy – as the final curtain fell on yet another contender's bid for the role of the Immortal Beloved.

NINE

Ghouls

*U*P TO DATE and back in Beethoven's lodgings the face of the dead man is now completely covered in plaster. Hovering over it is Danhauser, who taps the plaster to see if it has set. Evidently satisfied, he takes a firm grip on the mask and with both hands prises it off and gives a grunt of triumph.

'Got you this time, you slippery devil.'

'Death has taught him patience, Master,' Tantfl, his assistant, replies ingratiatingly.

'And cooled his temper,' gloats Danhauser. 'Prepare fresh plaster. I'm anxious to see the results.'

As Tantfl hastens to obey Danhauser blows away some of the loose plaster from within the mask in order to coat the surface with a fine layer of grease. Beethoven's own features still glisten from a similar application and give him the appearance of a man in a fever rather than a creature drained of life.

Meanwhile, in the next room Dr Warwuch is washing his autopsy instruments in a bowl and talking in low tones with Holtz and Schindler. 'Jaundice, haemorrhage, pneumonia and dropsy were all contributory factors, but it was cirrhosis of the liver that finally proved fatal.'

'Were you able to diagnose the cause of his deafness?' asks Schindler anxiously.

Without hesitation Dr Warwuch replies: 'Neuritis acoustica – atrophy of the acoustic nerve. Worse in the left ear. There's no known cure.' He throws the dirty water out of the window and dries his instruments with a dishcloth.

'But what caused it?' questions Holtz.

Dr Warwuch becomes a little uneasy, tentative. 'In his youth he suffered a serious bout of typhoid fever. The acoustic nerve is highly sensitive to the toxins of such a disease.'

'He always attributed his stomach ailments to the same cause,' says Schindler.

'He may well have been right,' admits the doctor. 'Now, if you will excuse me I must hurry while I can still get through the crowd outside.' Having placed the instruments in his bag, he slips into his coat, eager to be off. But Holtz is not satisfied.

'Isn't there another disease that can decay the nerves of hearing – cause deafness, doctor?'

Dr Warwuch will not be drawn into opening up a can of worms. 'Any further conclusion would be pure speculation. I must get to the Coroner's office. Have all the arrangements been made?'

Schindler nods. 'I shall remain here and supervise them personally.'

Schindler sees Dr Warwuch to the door, then returns to confront Holtz, who is far from satisfied with the doctor's report and is rapidly perusing the contents of the bookshelf.

'You seem dissatisfied with the doctor's diagnosis,' Schindler remarks. 'May I ask why?'

'Because I'm more familiar with the subject's case history than our good doctor,' says Holtz, still searching. 'I think his deafness was a symptom of a different disease entirely. Ah-ha!' He finds the volume he has been looking for and excitedly flicks through it. It falls open on a page evidently well read.

Schindler's curiosity gives way to alarm. 'What have you there?'

Holtz slaps the book into Schindler's hand. 'Well thumbed, you'll notice. A small treatise by L.V. Legunan . . .'

Schindler reads aloud with growing outrage: '"The Art of Recognizing and Curing All Venereal Infections" . . . The Master is not yet in his coffin and you are ready to sully his name, discredit his achievement – belittle his suffering!'

'And you are ready to canonize the man! Dear God, we already have a patron saint of music. What we need is a grubby, ill-tempered, ugly little man, who despite everything managed to show us the heavens through his music. And by God does this age need such an inspiration! You would lay a smoke-screen of platitudes, obscure the very mortality of such a man – diminish him. Schindler, you lived with the little terror, yet you don't seem to know him. I want to clear the air, see the complete man.'

'I know him well enough to know what his answer to that would be,' sneers Schindler. 'He'd tell you that you might as well go piss in the wind!'

Holtz momentarily admires him. 'There's hope for you yet, man!'

'Anyway, perhaps he got that book for his nephew Carl. He was constantly warning him about corrupt women.'

'"Prostitutes" is the word you want,' says Holtz bluntly. 'That might explain his abhorrence of the boy's mother. She was little better than a whore.' A fresh thought suddenly strikes him. 'Then there's this business of never marrying. Perhaps . . .'

'What madness are you about to hypothesize now?'

'We both know he loved children, and if, say, if there was a problem in that direction – if he was poxed,' says Holtz with a growing conviction that makes Schindler wince, 'what better than to marry into a ready-made family. Countess Erdody's, for example.'

Schindler is outraged. 'That's criminal. Really you are insane. She was deported!'

'You're putting the cart before the horse. That was much later,' replies Holtz with a smile. 'When she first took Beethoven in she was a paragon of virtue.'

'Separated from her husband!' sneers Schindler.

'But still married in law. In those letters of his to the Immortal Beloved he writes of an impediment. It could have been her husband.'

'Nonsense,' scoffs Schindler. 'He meant his deafness. And to suggest Beethoven would stoop to cuckolding – no, preposterous!'

'So he was a man of honour and a paragon of virtue, or that's what you'd have us believe. I believe differently. At heart he was a crafty opportunist and a shameless philanderer.'

Dr Warwuch, still hovering outside the door, curious to hear their comments, has heard enough and finally creeps away with a sad shake of his head. Can these two opinionated ghouls be discussing the same man?

TEN

Keyhole Comedy

A GOLDEN CORNUCOPIA ROLLS majestically over hill and dale drawn by twelve milk-white oxen. Flowers are interwoven in the spokes of the wheels, which turn in time to the expansive first movement of Beethoven's 'Pastoral' Symphony. Enthroned in the cornucopia and crowned with vine leaves, Bacchus rides triumphant. It is Beethoven, smiling and affable – a living personification of his generous music. Attending him are Greek youths and maidens, for this is a vision of Arcadia and Beethoven is their god. Peasant women gathering grapes pay him reverence; peasant men bringing in the harvest salute him. Children driving cattle and herding sheep laugh joyously and wave to him. Beethoven blesses them in turn – through his music. Now the vision is approaching a palace where a handsome woman awaits with three beautiful children atop a flight of stairs strewn with rose petals.

Ascending the stairs with his retinue, Beethoven is greeted with applause by the children and a warm embrace from the mother . . . who slowly awakes from her dream and stretches with a sensuous smile and for a moment wonders where she is. She listens acutely: no birdsong, but the rumble of traffic. So she is not at her mansion in the country but her stately residence in Vienna, 1074 Krugerstrasse to be precise. The lucky lady is none other than Maria, Countess Erdody, Hungarian, thirty years of age, mother of three, with large inviting eyes set in a pretty face that rarely sees the sunshine. Separated from her husband, she is rich, influential, a good pianist and a semi-invalid. Excited by her vivid dream, she must share it! Leaning out of bed, she lowers herself to the floor and drags her way across the carpet in her exquisite lace nightdress. The room itself is resplendent, with a magnificent grand piano and furnishings of great luxury that proclaim that the occupant spends much time there. Climbing into her wheelchair, she propels herself from the room and excitedly wheels herself down a corridor, past antique statues and sombre portraits of her ancestors. She is about to turn a corner when a voice makes her hesitate. She turns to see her ten-year-old son Fritzl peeping from behind his bedroom door.

'Mama, may I push you?'

'Fritzl! I've told you before, you are not to wander about at night.'

'But, Mama, it's morning.'

'Do as Mama tells you – immediately.'

She waits until he obeys her and closes the door behind him. Only then does she resume her journey towards a room from which snatches of piano music are issuing.

In his spacious suite Beethoven is sprawled, half dressed, across his bed. He has dragged his piano beside the bed and is working on the Choral Fantasia Op. 50, in which he is completely immersed and deaf to the world in more ways than one. Without ceremony Maria bursts in on him and starts shouting. He immediately loses the thread but nevertheless tries to continue working.

'Luigi, I must tell you of my dream!' insists Maria. 'Your "Pastoral" Symphony – the first movement – you were Bacchus in a golden cornucopia and all the peasants were paying homage to you, the God of Grapes.' She climbs on to the bed and snuggles up to him. 'Tell me, Luigi, is that how you see it? I've an intuitive feeling that it means something like that to you. Tell me. Am I right?'

'To me it means *allegro ma non troppo*,' he replies, resisting the temptation to kick her out of bed.

'Oh, Luigi, don't be so pedantic!' she scolds. 'No, don't turn your left ear to me! I *do* see you as Bacchus. He's quite the best god I know. Aren't you flattered?' Beethoven snorts and turns away, but Maria persists. 'Do you see *me* as a goddess, Luigi?'

Beethoven, still vainly trying to work, is more candid. 'At this moment I wish you were the goddess Angerona.'

'Angerona? Who's she?'

'The goddess of silence,' Beethoven replies flatly.

Maria explodes. 'Oh, you beast. I'm not Angerona, I'm Venus.' Half in anger, half in jest, she starts to tickle him. 'Say it, say I'm Venus, Venus, Venus. Say it.'

Unaware she's playing with a volcano, Maria is fortunate in that it only erupts in laughter.

'Venus. I capitulate. You're Venus.'

The manuscript on which Beethoven has been working slips to the floor as Maria pulls the covers over them. Even so they are under observation, for someone is looking through the keyhole. He is gawky and dressed in ill-fitting livery but has a roguish face creased in smiles. Around the corner lightly steps a handsome aristocrat in a dressing-gown, who stops dead in his tracks at the sight of the Peeping Tom. Then, creeping up quietly, the aristocrat grabs him by the ear and walks him briskly down the corridor. Young Fritzl, who has been spying, too, barely has time to duck back into his room before the two men bustle around the corner. Only then is the ear released. The two men come eye to eye. The aristocrat is Prince Lichnowsky, a wealthy landowner and patron of the arts; the liveried man is Spieler, a thirty-year-old Jack-of-all-trades and presently Beethoven's nosy servant. They talk in hushed tones.

'Now, do I take the liberal view and assume you simply do not know *how* to knock on a door,' demands the Prince, 'or, since your livery is not of this household, that you insinuated your way in here as a spy?'

'My master likes me close at hand at all times seeing he's deaf as a p . . . hard of hearing, sir,' comes the reply. 'I have the honour to serve Herr van Beethoven.'

All becomes clear. 'I have not been informed that he was here,' says the Prince sourly. 'When did Herr van Beethoven arrive?'

'You'll pardon me, sir,' replies Spieler with mock humility, 'but the last thing he told me was to button my lip. Who knows? I mean you might be one of those detestable snoopers from the *Vienna Daily Star*.'

The accusation rankles somewhat, but the Prince appreciates the servant's point. 'I hardly think so, fellow. I am well acquainted with your master. I am Prince Lichnowsky. He has surely mentioned my name?'

Spieler plays along. 'Forgive me many times, Your Highness. It was the dressing-gown – so humble for one so high-born, if I may say so – otherwise . . . Why, your name is ever on his lips, sir. Only yesterday . . .' He bites his lip.

'Indeed? Most gratifying,' says the Prince with a smile. 'I thought I was quite forgotten.' Then, quick as a flash, he catches Spieler's arm as he turns to go. 'What did he say? Beethoven and I have no secrets. He owes everything to me. Now speak out.'

Spieler replies reluctantly, 'He was telling me . . . well, not *me*, exactly . . .'

The Prince helps him out. 'You were close at hand, so to speak?'

Spieler nods thankfully and continues with fake servility. 'Yes, sire. Well, he was talking about the last occupation and how you ordered him to play for some French officers you were entertaining and he told you to . . . stuff it, whereupon you reminded him you were his social superior, to which he replied, "Prince, what you are, you are by accident of birth; what I am, I am through my own efforts. There have been and will be thousands of princes; there is only one Beethoven." I hope I quote correctly, Your Highness.'

'To the last syllable,' replies the Prince affably, while despising the latent arrogance of this loathsome underling. 'What is he doing here?'

The merest hint of contempt crosses Spieler's cheeky face, while further conversation is silenced by the sound of the door bumping open and the approach of a squeaky wheelchair.

In the nick of time the two men withdraw into the relative seclusion of a dusty arras as Maria sails by in her hand-driven chair. Spieler peeps out to see if the coast is clear and then gives an affirmative nod to the Prince, who emerges, his face thunderous, having become an unwitting accomplice to a highly detestable rogue bent on having the last word.

'If your Highness will pardon me, there is a smudge of dirt just below your beauty spot,' he points out, leaving the humiliated Prince to wipe it off. 'Just so, sir,' adds Spieler before backing off with a deep bow that leaves the Prince feeling distinctly inferior. Angrily, he stomps off in the opposite direction. Unobserved, little Fritzl watches the Prince knock on his mother's bedroom door and enter.

Maria is sitting up in bed enjoying a stein of ale as Prince Lichnowsky enters. She smiles and pats the counterpane invitingly. Kissing her hand, the Prince sits on the bed. Maria can see all is not well, so she greets him effusively.

'Kiki, what a lovely surprise! Why aren't you riding in the Josefstadt?'

'Because, my dear Mimi, your note asked me not to leave the house until I had seen you on a matter of great importance,' the Prince graciously replies, 'and this morning I have to leave for Graz.'

'But, Kiki, you have only just arrived,' Maria protests. 'Don't you like it here?'

'Putting an entire floor at my disposal is more than generous, Maria. You make my trips to Vienna a constant pleasure. But estate business calls me back.'

'What a pity! You'll miss Luigi's recital, and he plays so seldom these days.'

Immediately, the Prince's affability vanishes. 'I gather he is also enjoying your hospitality.'

'Oh, you've seen him then?' she exclaims in surprise.

'I met his servant, which is just as bad. Really, Maria, your house is turning into a veritable hospice for lame ducks – first that destitute cellist fellow and now Beethoven . . .'

'Oh, Kiki, I had to take him in. His place is positively roofless! I must tell you, I had gone for a lesson at his lodgings – and you know his curious habit of pouring water over his hands whenever he plays – well, he'd been doing that all morning, constantly instructing me by example. Poor Spieler was forever at the pump refilling the wash-basin – the floor was quite awash.'

'Yes, I, too, have suffered from Beethoven's compulsive behaviour,' mutters the Prince grimly.

But Maria hasn't finished. 'Then the door burst open and the landlord stood there shouting at the top of his voice. Apparently the plaster was dropping from his ceiling below, and the carpet was quite ruined!'

'Most amusing,' remarks the Prince, unsmiling.

'I haven't finished yet. Then the landlord shouted, "If I'd wanted the water music, I'd have sent for Handel," whereupon Luigi picked up the chamber pot and emptied it all over his head!' She laughs and gently takes the Prince's hand. 'Oh, you're not angry with me, Kiki? One feels some responsibility, and how his eyes lit up when he saw my library. He has such a thirst to better himself. It's quite touching to see. Say you're not angry.'

'I suppose I would have done the same thing. Not that he would have accepted my hospitality,' says the Prince dolefully.

'Oh, this silly rift between you two! Kiki, it has gone on far too long. He respects you – you did so much for him in the early days – all those pieces he dedicated to you, and then a stupid quarrel simply because he refuses to play for the French!'

'I am beginning to suspect the substance of your note,' says the Prince.

'An annuity,' blurts out Maria. 'If Beethoven could only be sure of a regular income it would do wonders for his peace of mind. He could settle down. You know how hopeless he is in business matters. He even suspects his publishers of cheating him, not to mention his servants.'

'For the pauper he is, he possesses inordinate pride. I doubt he would accept my patronage again, and as for his paranoia I can hardly bear responsibility for that.'

'I know, but you could use your influence with Prince Lobkowitz,' urges Maria, 'or the Archduke Rudolph, for example.'

'An epileptic and a deaf man – the mind balks.' The Prince raises his eyes to heaven. 'I shall be dining with Prince Kinsky tomorrow; I suppose I could mention it.'

'Splendid! There's not a moment to lose. You realize that he has been offered a post with the King of Westphalia?'

The Prince is astonished. 'Napoleon's brother? Never! He'd never accept that. At least his obstinacy is consistent.'

'So is his poverty. Six hundred gold ducats a year they're offering him, and only the lightest of duties, and the right to conduct whenever he pleases. I feel that once he is stolen away Vienna will never get him back.'

'He walked out on me, Maria; humiliated me in front of friends.'

'He is not of a class that understands diplomacy, Kiki. In his eyes you were fraternizing with the enemy and –'

'And now that it suits his pocket he's ready to do likewise. For years I've been waiting for an apology. Not a word.'

'He's a law unto himself. Come, Kiki, it's not like you to hold a grudge. Think what posterity will say.'

'No, Maria.'

'Not even for me?'

'Least of all for you. One day you'll thank me.'

Maria puts her arm around him, smiling seductively, and he is evidently swayed. She murmurs, 'Is there no way, dearest Kiki, that I can prevail upon you . . . ?'

He smiles in return as she pulls him towards her, little knowing that their secret liaison will soon be common knowledge. Yes, Spieler is spying through the keyhole again, enjoying himself enormously. Suddenly a footfall: someone is behind him. Quick as a flash Spieler has whipped out a kerchief from his pocket and is polishing the doorknob. Confronting him is a sallow-faced, flashily dressed woman in her mid-thirties holding in her arms a two-and-a-half-year-old child. The woman is Johanna, Beethoven's despised sister-in-law, and the child is her son Karl.

'How did you get in here?' hisses Spieler.

'I used the magic word: Beethoven!' she crows.

'Keep your voice down! You've no right to come here.'

'He wanted to see Karlie as soon as he got over his cough. Did you expect him to walk around by himself?'

'The Maestro's been up working all night, and now he's asleep.'

'Well, we'll have to wake the Maestro up then, won't we, Karlie darling?' she whispers to the child before bawling down the corridor, 'Ludwig! Where are you? I know your lugholes work when you want them to!'

'God in heaven, keep your voice down,' hisses Spieler. 'This isn't a whore-house.'

But Johanna ignores him. 'Hey, Ludwig! I see you brought your pimp with you! Where are you, brother-in-law of mine?' And she opens the nearest door – Maria's – and peeps in. An outraged scream, and she backs out again. 'I'm shocked,' says Johanna dryly.

'The Master will never forgive you for this!' exclaims a fraught Spieler.

Before she can collect herself Johanna is confronted by a furious Countess Maria.

'What is the meaning of this outrage? Spieler, fetch the militia! Who is this person?'

'This person can speak for herself,' butts in the intruder before Spieler can reply. 'I'm Frau Beethoven.'

Suddenly a roar turns everyone to stone. 'Spieler! Where the hell are you? Where's that coffee?'

With a nod that suffices for a bow, Spieler is off down the corridor and around the corner to face his irate master, leaving the two women to size each other up. It doesn't take long. Maria takes Johanna for a troublemaker, while Johanna sees easy pickings.

'What can I say, Countess? I'm more sorry than I can say. The lower orders always bring out the worst in me. But I have business with my brother-in-law.'

Maria is suspicious. 'Your business must be very urgent to bring you here at this hour – with a child, too. She looks ill.'

'*He* is. Poor little Karlie, he needs a tonic,' whines Johanna, 'but then medicines cost money, don't they, precious?'

'But surely your husband . . . ?'

'Alas, an invalid, too. Runs in the family. I hate to trouble Ludwig when he's working, but we are in great trouble, and then he *has* provided for us as long as I can remember.' She starts edging towards Beethoven's room. 'So, begging your pardon, I'll just –'

Maria knows she is being blackmailed, but no price is too high for Beethoven's peace of mind. 'No!' she exclaims. 'Luigi is not enjoying the best of health either. *I* will be only too happy to help you through this difficult period – providing Beethoven himself is not burdened. Do you understand?'

'Perfectly, my lady,' Johanna replies apparently with deep humility as she surreptitiously pinches baby Karl, who begins to cry. 'Hush, pet,' she croons. 'The nice lady will see you don't go hungry.'

And for Beethoven's sake Maria gives in. 'Of course he won't. Just leave your address and I'll see that –'

But once again the sound of Beethoven's distant voice freezes them into silence. 'Then you *should* have done it! Off with you, and be sharp about it. There may be hundreds waiting there!'

'Of course, Master, right away!' comes the muffled reply, which is followed by the sound of a door opening in the adjacent corridor and the voice of Beethoven mumbling obscenities.

Maria turns hastily to Johanna. 'Quick, down the backstairs. You must not be seen!' She indicates a nearby door.

Johanna hesitates. 'Spieler knows my address.'

'Yes! Yes!' whispers Maria. 'Now hurry. Go!'

As Johanna disappears down the backstairs Maria quickly opens the bedroom door and waves to the Prince to be patient. Then, swiftly closing it, she spins about to face Beethoven as he rounds the corner. He is obviously heading for her bedroom but is forced to retrace his steps as Maria wheels her way past him down the corridor.

'Servants! Pah! Thieves! Cheats! Swindlers!' he rants. 'The last one thought I couldn't tell there were only forty beans to my coffee instead of sixty; this one bills me for sirloin and serves me scrag-end! Not only does he eat like a bottom-less pit, he has a memory like a bottomless pit!'

'You'll never have to worry about domestic matters ever again, Luigi,' Maria reassures him.

But he doesn't hear her and rambles on. 'And on top of it all he forgot to post a change of address sign outside my old lodgings – and with my grand gala concert almost upon us. There will be queues a mile long and that blasted landlord won't tell 'em I've moved on because he's still wiping shit off his face.'

Maria stops. Beethoven carries on a few paces, then pauses as he realizes she's speaking.

'What *are* you talking about, Luigi?'

'The tickets! For my concert appearance, naturally!'

'But what about them?'

'I sell them.'

'From your home?' asks Maria in dismay.

'From *your* home now, since that *is* where I live,' he replies emphatically.

'But, but, Luigi – whatever for?'

'Promoters! Can't trust 'em! All thieves! Any corner near the front door will do.'

Fortunately Maria is learning to accept his paradoxical behaviour. 'Of course, Luigi.'

'Oh, and I'll need somewhere to store a few bits and pieces that'll be arriving some time. The furniture.'

Totally under his spell she can only repeat, 'Of course.' Then she catches sight of Fritzl lurking in his doorway, annoyed that he has witnessed her humiliation. 'Fritzl, stop dithering! It's time you were washed and dressed.'

'Yes, Mama,' he replies with a sly grin to Beethoven.

Beethoven grins back. 'Ha! Have at you, little Hungarian sausage!' Playfully he boxes him. Fritzl is delighted; not so his mother.

'Fritzl!'

'Yes, Mama, I'm going. Goodbye, Captain!'

This is obviously the continuation of a game because Beethoven salutes and clicks his heels as he replies, '*Au revoir, Mon Général!* Quick march!'

As the boy stomps off to his room Beethoven beams with pleasure: 'Ha! He likes me. See that? He likes me.'

'He does indeed,' replies Maria, genuinely moved. 'You could be a second father to him, Luigi.'

'Quite, quite,' says Beethoven, cooling a little. 'But now it's time to get down to business. It's time to build a box office.'

'Of course, Luigi,' Maria replies, feigning an enthusiasm she is far from feeling. In all her experience she's never had such a demanding house guest – but then she's never had to entertain a genius before.

As things transpire, Maria has to suffer the humility of babbling queues outside her front door only for a few days, for well before the night of the gala on 22 December 1808 every ticket had been sold. The billboard outside the Theater an der Wien boldly proclaims 'Standing Room Only'. As Beethoven launches the orchestra into the first performance of his Choral Fantasia the entire audience, feeling extremely privileged, is keyed up to witness a truly momentous occasion.

And so it proves to be, though not in the manner they had anticipated, for the sound they hear is like an orchestra tuning up – sheer cacophony. Maria is almost in tears while the rest of the audience reacts with varying degrees of laughter and pathos.

Beethoven at the piano, oblivious to the orchestra and singers trying valiantly to stay with him, hears the music in his head as beautiful and melodic, but everyone else hears the reality. So delicately does he caress the keys in the soft passages that no chords sound, while in the heavier sections he mangles the piano so brutally that it is discordant and ugly – indeed, some strings are broken. He plays with his eyes shut, interpreting the music through his body with his ear close to the keys. Eventually he does open his eyes and ultimately homes in on Prince Lichnowsky, who is sniggering. He also sees Fritzl sitting stock still, eternally loyal to him. But by now all the composer can hear is the hum and buzz of his own ears and the insistent laughter of Lichnowsky – amplified a hundred times in his imagination. The orchestra ends a beat or so after Beethoven has finished. With dignity he rises, looks at the audience and leaves. He will never play in public again. This is his last appearance as a concert pianist.

ELEVEN

The Sphinx

THE MUSIC ROOM in Maria's house is also a library, light and airy. A harp stands in the corner and a grand piano with closed lid in the middle, on which Beethoven is stretched like a reclining sphinx. His great paws coax a strange melody from the keyboard. Stranger still, he has a large silk handkerchief draped over his head. Maria's children stand around him as still as statues, vaguely Egyptian. Fritzl, eleven, poses on the windowsill with arms outstretched like a bird. Mimi, eight, stands before the fire holding a lighted candle in each outstretched hand, while Gusti, ten, holds a curtain tassel serving as a tail in one hand and a live mouse in the other, which she contemplates like a Cheshire cat.

The tableau is mysterious, bizarre and unexpected – at least to Maria, as she bursts into the room in her wheelchair.

'Good grief! What on earth are you doing? Fritzl, get down immediately! People will think the house is on fire. And it *will* be ablaze if you don't put out those candles, Mimi. Gusti, what are you doing to that poor mouse? Put it back in the cage immediately. I thought this was supposed to be a music lesson.' Maria snatches the candles from Mimi, while Gusti returns the mouse to its cage.

'It *is* a music lesson, Mama,' Gusti insists. 'I'm Baast, Goddess of Pleasure. She was an Egyptian cat – well, half cat, half human. And Mimi is Maat, the Goddess of Fire.'

'Wrong as usual!' says Fritzl. 'She's Sekhmet. Maat's the Goddess of Truth. And I'm Horus the falcon, the Sky God.'

Gusti turns to Maria. 'Ludwig found one of your books on Egypt.'

'We've been playing gods,' explains Mimi.

By now Maria has got over her surprise and is entering into the spirit of things. 'Heavens, Bacchus this morning . . . what is he this afternoon, pray?'

'Don't you know?' says Fritzl, 'We know he's –'

'Let me guess,' interrupts Maria. And as Beethoven plays on, oblivious, Maria wheels herself over to the piano. 'Behold! The Sphinx!'

The children are delighted and squeal approval. But there is no reaction from Beethoven, which makes Maria a trifle vexed.

'He is the *Great* Sphinx of Gizeh,' says Fritzl solemnly. 'No mortal has ever lifted his veil.'

'He dares you to lift it,' says Gusti to her mother.

'Fritzl says something terrible will happen if you do,' warns Mimi.

'The choice is yours,' says Fritzl.

'Shall I? Dare I? What would we do if Luigi began to spit fire and turned into a salamander?'

'That's Greek, not Egyptian,' says Fritzl. 'And he doesn't like being called Luigi. His name is Ludwig.'

Maria is perturbed by his obvious communion with Beethoven. 'Well, I don't think you need snap at Mama, darling.'

Despite the fact that this is a game Maria is undecided whether to accept the challenge or not. Suddenly more seems at stake than a simple dare. Should she strip the sphinx bare and risk divine wrath, or would it be more prudent to leave the secret behind the veil, unprobed. Yesterday she would have torn off the mask without a thought; today she hesitates.

'Perhaps he has no face,' says Fritzl, at which Mimi bursts into tears.

'Please, Mama, please, don't do it. I don't want you to!'

Maria comforts her: 'There, there, dearest. Of course I won't do it. I couldn't, anyway. No one has ever solved the secret of the . . . sphinx.'

'I could,' boasts Fritzl.

'You wouldn't. You're afraid,' says Gusti.

'Shall I, Mother?' asks Fritzl.

'Why not?' Maria laughs. 'If the idea of being turned to stone doesn't frighten you.'

Fritzl hesitates.

Gusti chides, 'Ha – little mouse!'

But for Maria the game has become tiresome. 'Enough of this nonsense. Luigi is obviously not feeling up to a lesson today. Run and get dressed. We're going on a nice outing.'

As the children run boisterously from the room, Maria turns back to

Beethoven, still inscrutable behind the kerchief. Maria addresses him in a loud voice. 'I cannot imagine what relevance you felt this peculiar demonstration has, but if you deign to step down from your pedestal and join us, we are going on a nice outing.' Beethoven does not move. 'Luigi, this is becoming childish.' Still no response. 'Oh, really! We're going on a picnic. So are you coming or not?'

Beethoven continues playing but declaims in a loud voice from under the kerchief, 'I am that which is. I am all that was, that is and shall be. No mortal has ever lifted my veil.'

Confused and exasperated, Maria wheels herself from the room accompanied by a crescendo of delirious chords. She bangs the door of the music room behind her, wheels herself away, stops, wheels back again, looks through the keyhole and sees the veiled sphinx continuing to play. But now he is wearing a top hat. Slowly he turns and raises his hat to her.

Maria laughs nervously. 'He's mad!' And though she continues laughing she feels uncomfortable, caught out.

TWELVE

High

*A*PICTURESQUE PROCESSION MAKES its way through gently falling rain along the shore of an Austrian lake. Striding ahead, unmindful of the wet, is Beethoven, hands tucked beneath his coat, a battered top hat tilted back to leave his brow bare to the elements, while in his head the elusive spirit of his Fifth Symphony struggles to take shape. A few steps behind him two footmen carry a sedan-chair containing a single passenger, Maria. She sips amber liquid from a glass phial and smiles at the rain, which to her looks like falling diamonds. A second chair follows, carrying the children, while Spieler and another servant bring up the rear with the picnic basket.

As the party passes through a grove of willows, Maria notices that Beethoven seems preoccupied by the raindrops falling from leaf to leaf (echoed in the music by gentle *pizzicato* strings). Beethoven slackens his pace, and the small cavalcade slows down also. Is his music imitating nature? Does he faintly hear the actual sound of rain on leaves? And that muffled beating is surely no drumbeat but the thump of his own heart? Has the impossible happened? From his expression there can be no doubting it. Everything seems to catch its breath, even his music falls silent seemingly poised on the brink, as Beethoven gives vent to his joy.

'I can hear it – the rain! I can hear it! My heart! I can hear it beating!'

Maria, who has watched this marvel, leaps from her chair and runs through the rain to embrace Beethoven deliriously . . . in her mind.

In reality she is still sitting in the sedan-chair, her eyes closed, a blissful smile on her lips. Once again she throws open the door and runs towards him. Barely has she hobbled a few agonizing steps when she collapses into the mud with a scream.

He reacts first and runs to assist, and as he lifts her to the shelter of a towering oak tree he shouts commandingly over his shoulder, 'A splendid spot. We'll picnic here! General, deploy your troops.'

The servants set down their burden, and the children run off to play hide-and-seek. Beethoven gently lowers the distraught Maria against the trunk of the tree.

'Oh, Luigi, I had a vision. You were listening to the raindrops. I ran towards you.'

He lifts the phial from her hand, removes the stopper, takes a sip and identifies the liquid as laudanum, an addictive pain-killing drug, available over the counter of every apothecary in the land. Beethoven responds with a quip and a shake of the head, 'Laudanum fantasia, tut-tut.'

'It makes you forget pain,' says Maria by way of explanation.

'And makes coming down to earth all the harder. Are you in pain now?' asks Beethoven gently.

'No. I didn't upset you, did I?' Maria is rapidly gaining control of herself, as he smiles and deftly wipes away a tear.

'From where I stood, you upset yourself – diving into the mud like that.'

'No, I meant in reminding you . . . Don't you ever dream of hearing your music again?'

Beethoven regards her with real sympathy. 'In a way I do hear it, all the time. I sometimes think it is everybody else who is deaf. Don't you dance and run,' he asks, touching her temple, 'in here?'

'Oh, how I used to before little Fritzl was born! Afterwards my legs and feet swelled like balloons. But in my dreams I'm dancing, running . . . If only we could convert dreams to waking reality!'

'It can be arranged,' he replies, hurling the phial into the lake, as Maria looks at him uncomprehendingly. 'My Christmas present to you. My dear, what are we? A small dot, little more than a speck – time can flick us off its arm in a trice. A hundred years from now people will hear my gift to you and see Maria Erdody dancing like no other. You shall have it on Christmas Day.'

'The three wise men came bearing gifts,' says Maria with a smile, as Beethoven kisses her hand.

'Ah, who can recall their names?' he replies, pointing across the lake to a shaggy donkey in a field. 'He's the one we remember.'

Maria gives way to laughter, her confidence restored.

THIRTEEN

Misconduct

*T*HE MUSIC ROOM is dark and cosy when the happy day eventually arrives, and Maria is about to enjoy her Christmas present with her daughters by her side. Fritzl proudly turns the pages for Beethoven at the piano, who, accompanied by a violinist and a cellist, is playing by candle-light – well and harmoniously this time, for he is among friends and his fellow musicians are following him.

Snow dances outside the windows, and Maria feels she is dancing, too. The Trio in D major is all Beethoven promised it to be – the most treasured gift she can ever have. In the eyes of Beethoven shines real gladness. Even Spieler, standing in the shadows, is aware of the enchantment in the air. It seems that Beethoven has at last found his beloved, and their joy is eternal. Or is it?

Bang! Beethoven slams the door behind him as he storms out of the house.

Behind him, the voice of Maria can be heard crying out in desperation. 'Luigi! Luigi, come back. *Luigi!*'

But Beethoven, untidy, hatless, half dressed and in great distress, ignores her. Some of the music under his arm spills on to the ground.

As he stoops to gather it up Maria peers over an upstairs balcony, Spieler at her side. They are equally upset. Maria shouts down at him. 'That was an absurd accusation, Luigi. Come back this instant and retract it.'

'I shall never set foot in your house again,' he yells back.

'Indeed you will *not*,' she replies with equal vehemence, 'unless you apolo-gize this instant!'

'Apologize? Ha!' Angrily, he turns on his heel.

'But where will you go?'

'Out of *this* perfumed garden. You never know who the snake in the grass is!'

On the balcony Spieler shouts after him: 'Master! Please.'

'Silence!' says Maria, lowering her voice. 'Please . . .'

'I'll run after him,' says Spieler, 'explain that the money he saw you giving me was for little Karlie.'

'No,' snaps Maria. 'If he chooses to think the worst of me, let him go. I have my pride, too.'

Spieler sees it is useless to protest.

Maria is crying. 'Take me inside. It's cold. Where will he go?'

'It's best a lady like you should not know.'

Spieler gently assists her back inside. They are both unaware that from a window on the floor above young Fritzl is sadly watching the receding figure of Beethoven. There are tears in the boy's eyes, too. Little does he guess that his hero is making for the local brothel in the hope of finding peace in the solitude of a whore's bedroom.

When Beethoven does enter such a refuge he still looks as wretched as a fish out of water. Behind him comes the madam, plump and pleasant, echoing the garish style of the room in her mode of dress.

'Elsa's sick. You can have her room, sir.' Beethoven reacts to the word 'sick', but the madam quickly reassures him. 'Nothing catching, sir, I assure you. She's just done her back in.'

Beethoven nods.

The madam probes a little. 'Trouble with the landlady again?'

'Took a fancy to my servant.'

She nods sympathetically, notices he's shivering. 'Make yourself at home,' she says with a knowing smile. 'I'll send something along to warm you up.'

Beethoven blankly watches her go. He looks at his music, sorts through it and comes to the title page. He reads it aloud, 'Trio in D major, dedicated to Countess Maria Erdody, Christmas 1808.' He looks at himself in the mirror. 'Got your fingers burned again, didn't you, Looooeeegi?'

He crosses to the fire, crushes the page into a ball and throws it on the flames. He watches it burn with the same disillusionment that he watched his dedication to Napoleon go up in smoke. He looks hopelessly into the flames for an answer.

Twenty years later, back in Beethoven's lodging, the answer to his question is still being pondered. And as usual there are two points of view.

'He was wrong to think her guilty of misconduct,' says Holtz, looking out of the window at the falling snow.

Schindler stops his note-taking to score a point off his rival. 'What would *you* have thought if you'd walked into a room unexpectedly and seen her sitting up in bed and handing your servant a large sum of money?' says Schindler. 'You'd have thought her guilty, too.'

And though both men continue their search in the hope of finding further hidden treasures they continue to argue like two dogs worrying a bone.

'In the event, she was merely guilty of protecting him,' claims Holtz. 'Presumably he found that out for himself eventually, because he apologized and she forgave him.'

'Six years later,' points out Schindler

'He'd have waited. She did a lot for him. That annuity, for instance – 12,000 florins.'

'Two weeks after he received it inflation rendered it worthless,' says Schindler.

'Hardly her fault,' snaps Holtz. 'Her intentions were most laudable, and Fate didn't exactly shine kindly on her. Fritzl died –'

'Under *very* mysterious circumstances, and Mimi attempts suicide,' adds Schindler, 'yet you still say the lady had no skeletons in her cupboard?'

'All I am saying is that rumour often becomes inextricable from fact,' says Holtz defensively.

'Rumour also has it that at least two of her servants enjoyed her bed,' gloats Schindler.

'Backstairs gossip!'

But Schindler loves rubbing it in. 'Beethoven belonged to the backstairs, perhaps he wasn't far off the mark after all. Where's there's smoke . . .'

Holtz winces at the platitude.

Schindler pauses to make notes, while Holtz becomes philosophical. 'If it had worked out the future would have been very promising. A pity. She seemed the one. Can't think of a better match.'

'You will, Holtz, you will,' says Schindler sarcastically.

His associate is still searching for a smart reply when Danhauser, the mask-maker, pokes his head around the door.

'Our work is finished here. We're leaving.'

'Did you get a satisfactory cast?' asks Schindler.

'The mould is excellent. Unfortunately the cast cracked.'

'Inferior clay,' says Holtz with a smile.

'Nonsense, my good sir!' says Danhauser, flaring. 'I use only the very best quality.'

'I meant inferior to the original,' says Holtz.

'I've got no time for sarcasm, sir,' Danhauser replies. 'I'll bid you goodbye, gentlemen. Come, Tantfl. I'll carry the mould myself.'

'Yes, master,' replies the obsequious Tantfl. 'Can I keep the razor I shaved him with?'

'Why not!'

As the two men hustle out Holtz wanders through the door into the next room. The cast of the death mask lies in pieces in a bucket. Holtz picks them up and begins to reassemble them on the table. A noise from Schindler makes him turn around.

'Still trying to make the pieces fit?'

'This one's easy. It's a mask.'

Together they look at the assembled cast.

'*Your* puzzle's all square pegs and round holes,' mocks Schindler.

'There's one round peg somewhere, Schindler, and I'm going to find it,' retorts Holtz, determinedly.

FOURTEEN

The Wrong Malfatti

*T*HERE IS A brief knock on the door, which is opened to reveal a sharp-faced, distinguished-looking man in his late fifties: Dr Malfatti.

'I hope I do not intrude, gentlemen. I'd hoped to be present at the autopsy.' He glances at the corpse and continues before they can reply. 'Ah! Too late, I see. Excuse me. In life one tries to help a patient, but, of course, one always wishes one could look underneath the cover, so to speak.'

He conducts a cursory examination.

'Hmm ... yes ... Warwuch did a thorough job, I see. Be interesting to compare notes, as it were.'

Holtz and Schindler exchange glances.

'He left some time ago,' says Holtz, slightly sickened by the prodding. 'We'll, er, leave you alone for a few moments.' He tugs Schindler by the sleeve through the doorway into the next room. Quietly he closes the door and whispers excitedly to his disgruntled rival, 'Enter one round peg!'

'Dr Malfatti?' Schindler is puzzled.

'His niece, Elise!' Holtz is triumphant. 'It's quite obvious! You know as well as I do that she was positively the last woman he ever proposed to.'

Schindler is annoyed that this possibility had not occurred to him.

'Elise Malfatti – your Immortal Beloved? It's no secret he was deeply smitten with her, I grant you, but ... I just don't know.'

'But *he* must know,' says Holtz.

'Then why don't you ask him?' mocks Schindler, indicating the closed door.

'I shall,' says Holtz, all bravado. He briskly opens the door.

*

Twenty years earlier in the same lodgings Beethoven is seated at the piano putting the finishing touches to his pop tune 'Für Elise'. Absent-mindedly he sips his coffee, grimaces and gives vent to his anger.

'Yaach! Noni! *Noni!* Can I not procure one decent, sober servant in this entire city? *Noni!*' As he looks towards the door he catches sight of the clock, which reads five minutes to three, and leaps to his feet. 'My God! She'll be here any minute. Noni. My cravat – is it washed and pressed? Where the hell is it?'

He rushes about the place in a panic, looking for the servant and the cravat. At that moment Noni, a plain middle-aged woman, enters carrying a shopping basket.

'My cravat – where is it?' he yells.

'In your wardrobe, sir,' she replies, flustered.

'Wardrobe? Wardrobe? Keep it on the hat rack in future.'

He flicks the cravat off the peg and begins to tie it in front of a cracked mirror, while Noni bustles about the place putting away groceries. She is obviously frightened of her new master.

'The coffee tastes like weak cow slurry. When I ask for sixty beans to the cup I mean sixty. Give me the key to the coffee box. I'll keep it in future.' She hands him the key. 'And no padding the bill – I know how much things cost.'

'Your sister-in-law was down the market asking again. And the pawnbroker says the pipe was only common Rhine craft, not ivory.' She replaces it in the pipe rack. 'And the baker says no more bread till the bill's paid.'

Suddenly conscious of the sad state of his wardrobe Beethoven hasn't heard a word. 'How much would a coat like this cost nowadays?'

Off a scarecrow, nothing, Noni thinks to herself.

'How much?' demands Beethoven.

'A brand-new coat would cost around fifty ducats, sir.'

Beethoven is outraged. 'Robbery! Fifty ducats! What can we do without, Noni?'

He takes a fat pencil from his pocket and starts scribbling on one of the shutters. This is his accounting board, scrawled with figures and graffiti. He thinks aloud. 'Taxes . . . paper money . . . redemption bonds . . . Debits: rent, a thousand; Karlie's doctor, medicines . . . hmmm; last two concerts – loss: a hundred, fifty. Your wages – God in heaven! – five thousand seven hundred and eight! Money that is owed to *me*: Fat King George of England, sixty guineas; Prince Kinsky and company, five thousand ducats – and I can spit in the wind for that. I'm owed five thousand six hundred ducats. Balance: one hundred and eight – in the red. Hmm!' He looks in the mirror again. 'I'm afraid, dear Elise, you'll have to take a ragged suitor.' On appraising his reflection he is not pleased and begins to doubt his image as a dashing lover. 'Noni! How old would you say I look?' He turns to face her. She's on the spot, diffident, nervous. 'Give me the truth. Loudly and clearly,' he insists.

'I dunno, sir, really I don't.'

'Come on, I won't be angry. Well? Would you say I was twenty-something?' She laughs. 'Well then, early thirties?'

'Oh, sir!'

'*Late* thirties. Hmm! My complexion . . . er, skin. What of that? How does that strike you?'

Noni sees this is not a game but something far more serious. Accordingly, she takes it seriously herself. 'Well, sir, you haven't been well lately – the colic and that. And I must say, sir, you don't eat regular – two or three days without a bite. Then the blockade and the rationing.'

'I take it you do not think much of my complexion! Well, so be it! What would you say *were* my redeeming features?'

'Redeeming?'

'What *attracts* you, for God's sake!'

'Attract? Why, sir, in my place I never think such thoughts.'

Beethoven gently takes her hand: 'Think them now, please. I need help.'

Noni is reassured. 'The eyes. You've got good eyes, sir.'

'Eyes . . . good! They're the windows of the soul, Noni!' He throws his spectacles into a corner. (He never wears them again.) 'Now we're getting somewhere,' he says with growing confidence. 'Can you dance?'

Noni is getting over her surprise and beginning to accept this as the normal behaviour of an artist. 'I used to polka, sir, in the village.'

Beethoven approaches her, bows and offers his arm. 'May I have the pleasure?'

Noni enters into the spirit of the fantasy, curtsies and joins him in the dance. Beethoven, curiously, could never keep time, and his efforts are clumsy. He is, however, eager to learn, and Noni does her best.

'No, sir. *One*-two-three, *one*-two-three,' she says, trying to help. 'Good, sir. Now you got it!'

He treads on her toe. She stifles a yell but winces.

'Hopeless!' Beethoven is despondent. 'Go and stand over there.'

He almost pushes her into a corner, then walks to the farthest side of the room and turns his back to her. 'Now say something to me. Speak to me – anything, small talk like the gentry would. Don't shout, just normal.'

After a pause she manages to summon up courage. 'Innit nice?' Seeing no response, she speaks up. 'Innit nice, NOW THE SNOW'S GAWN?'

After a slight pause Beethoven turns to face her. 'You did say something?' he queries.

She nods her head in affirmation. Clearly he heard nothing. Beethoven looks very vulnerable. Noni's face softens with sympathy.

'Say it again.'

Noni dutifully obliges: 'Innit nice, now the snow's –'

Beethoven does his best. 'Crows?'

'No, snow's,' says Noni faintly, before articulating every word loud and clear. 'Innit nice, now the snow's gawn?' And she gives him a smile of encouragement.

'Don't look at me like that,' snaps Beethoven. 'I can't stand your pity! Do anything – laugh if you must – but . . . Look, isn't it funny?' And with a flourish he produces an object from his back pocket. 'It's called an ear trumpet. Didn't know I played the trumpet, did you? That's a joke. Laugh! Isn't it funny?'

'No, sir. It's not funny,' says Noni gravely.

'Get out! Get out!' says Beethoven, fuming.

Noni runs out, as hurt and upset as her master, only to return, breathless, a moment later. 'Master, there's someone to see you called Malfatti.'

Beethoven pulls himself together, smoothes his hair, straightens his cravat and tucks his frayed shirt cuffs up his coat sleeves. At last he looks as good as he's ever going to look.

'Show her in! Hurry!'

Noni frowns, goes to say something, judges it more prudent not to and leaves the room. The door swings closed behind her. Beethoven swiftly seats himself at the piano and begins to play the highly romantic 'Für Elise'. He is very nervous.

The smile of anticipation on his face quickly fades as the door opens to reveal not Elise but her uncle Dr Johann Malfatti, diffident and a bit of a dandy. Beethoven stops playing and gets to his feet in confusion.

'Oh, doctor! I wasn't expecting . . . Er, my colic's cleared up.'

Dr Malfatti removes his hat, does his best to look nonchalant. 'Forgive my calling unannounced.'

'It's just that I'm expecting a pupil,' mumbles Beethoven.

'My niece is unable to come. She asked me to give you this.' The doctor attempts a little levity. 'I don't usually act as postman, but as she knew I was coming . . .' He hands a sealed letter to Beethoven, who takes it like an automaton. 'She is sure that all will become clear,' says the doctor with growing discomfort, 'er, when you have had time to digest the, er, contents.' He gets lost and starts again. 'She has gone away for an indefinite period of time.'

'Gone? Away?' says Beethoven uncomprehendingly.

'Yes. To a spa. I'm bound to say it was upon my recommendation, both as her doctor and her –' Dr Malfatti strives to gain control.

'A spa,' says Beethoven, interrupting. 'Is she ill? She was perfectly well last Thursday.'

'It's nothing serious,' replies the doctor reassuringly. 'She will soon be herself again. I'm more concerned about you. I'd like to give you a thorough examination.'

Beethoven is speechless. His world is falling apart.

'You have to be well to work,' says the doctor. 'I know that is the most important thing in life to you.'

'She left on your recommendation, you say?' says Beethoven, completely at a loss. 'But you looked me over last week.'

'As a result of which I'd value a second opinion.' The doctor goes to the door. 'Dr Dorner, would you come in, please?'

A moment later a bespectacled, plump little man appears at Dr Malfatti's side.

'Dr Dorner, may I introduce Herr Ludwig van Beethoven.' He turns to Beethoven. 'Dr Dorner is a specialist in pathogenesis, a subject close to my heart.'

'It is an honour, sir.' Dr Dorner smiles ingratiatingly.

Beethoven begins to collect himself. 'Patho . . . ? What's that? Moral support?'

'Pathogenesis is the science of tracing diseases back to their origin.'

Beethoven holds up a single finger. 'Like blaming my deafness on a pimple on my forefinger.'

Dr Malfatti is getting impatient. 'If you would just undress, we will not keep you long.'

'You'll not keep me at all,' says Beethoven calmly. He rolls up the sheet of music on the piano and ties it with a piece of string. 'Fate is the cause of my deafness, doctor. Any other bodily ailments are my own business.' He hands the scroll to Dr Malfatti. 'This is for your niece. You know the address, "Mr Postman". Goodbye!'

Malfatti protests vehemently. 'Beethoven, she's eighteen years old. You're –'

'Forty-one or so, too old for any more examinations,' interrupts Beethoven. 'I've been under your magnifying glass too long, it seems to me.'

'How can I help you if you won't cooperate,' says Dr Malfatti with growing anger. 'I wash my hands of you!'

'I'm not ready to lie down yet,' says Beethoven firmly.

Whereupon Dr Malfatti turns on his heel and stamps out of the room, leaving Dr Dorner standing uncomfortably in the doorway.

'Well, I'm also a busy man, and if you won't –'

Beethoven explodes. 'Quacks! All of you! Get out!'

FIFTEEN

The Note

A S HE EXAMINES the corpse of his reluctant patient Dr Malfatti recalls this incident with grim satisfaction. He looks around with a start at the sound of a voice.

'Dr Malfatti.' Holtz has crept up behind him. 'I would like to ask you something of a rather personal nature.'

'What is it?'

'Was there any further contact between Beethoven and your niece after May 1810?' Dr Malfatti is taken aback. Holtz continues, 'I ask not out of any malicious curiosity, but...' he glances over his shoulder at Schindler, who is also taking an interest in the conversation, before continuing, '... shortly before he died he entrusted me personally with his official biography.'

This is news to Schindler, who is deeply shocked and gives vent to a bellow of rage. Holtz carries on, unmoved.

'And in view of certain documents that have come to light I am most anxious to –'

'Beethoven dispensed with my services many years ago,' says Dr Malfatti coldly. 'Recently he saw fit to reconsider that decision. It is unethical to discuss a patient with anybody, official or otherwise, Herr Holtz. And my niece has been a respectable married woman these last ten years, I'll have you know.'

'Forgive me, I beg of you,' says Holtz apologetically. 'May I ask you just one further question? Have you determined the cause of Beethoven's deafness? I'm familiar with your treatise on pathogenesis, and it would be most enlightening to hear your opinion.'

Though flattered, Dr Malfatti refuses to be drawn. 'It would be more germane to the matter if you speak to Dr Warwuch. He conducted the official autopsy. Good day.' And he is gone before Holtz can protest.

Schindler, who is seething with suppressed fury, finally explodes. 'Your obsession is now clear. Crystal clear! *And* your motive for picking my brains! Have you a publisher in mind? Or a title, perhaps? What about *Beloved Thief?*'

Holtz, temper frayed, spins around and grabs Schindler by the lapels. 'Listen, you sycophantic ghoul! I said he *entrusted* me with it, that's all. As for picking your brains, I'll leave that to the maggots!' He releases his hold on Schindler, who is speechless. 'I leave the dead to bury the dead.' So saying, Holtz collects his hat and hurries from the room.

For a moment Schindler continues to stare after him, then starts to search feverishly for the Immortal Beloved letters. Drawing a blank, he hurries to the door and calls down the stairs, 'Holtz! Bring them back! Holtz! Stop, thief!' There is no reply, so running back into the room in frustration he shouts at Beethoven, 'He's run off with the bloody love letters!' Immediately realizing the folly of his remark, he looks at his dead master guiltily. Beethoven stares back, enigmatic as ever.

Meanwhile, in the darkening street outside knots of people hang about, glancing up from time to time at Beethoven's window. At the front door Fanny Del Rio, a small, rather plain woman in her early thirties, is arguing with a militiaman. She is a schoolteacher and one of the few women who enjoyed a platonic relationship with Beethoven, or so she would have us believe. Her worried features suddenly lighten at the appearance of Holtz on his way out.

'Oh, Karl, thank goodness. I knew you were up there, but this 'ere cop wouldn't let me in because I didn't have permission from you. I said I couldn't get permission from you without I go up and see you, and since −'

'Just carrying out your instructions, sir,' says the militiaman, interrupting. 'She's not on the official list you gave me.'

'Very remiss of me, Constable. She should have been. Fanny, forgive me.'

'Oh, that's all right. I'm used to it, sir.'

Holtz looks contrite as she pushes past him and runs up the stairs.

'I kept away the press like you said, sir,' says the militiaman. 'Is there anyone else I should know about?'

'No, there's no one else.'

Holtz presses some coins into the constable's hand, turns his collar up against the chill wind and hurries through the scattered crowd into the fading March twilight. A shady-looking man lurking near by follows him. A moment later he taps Holtz on the shoulder and slips him a note. Recovering from his surprise, Holtz reads it as they turn into an alley so as to be unobserved.

'Did she mention her name, the woman who gave you this?' asks Holtz eagerly.

The man shrugs. '"Just give it to Herr Holtz," was all she said. She gave me ten ducats.'

'What did she look like?'

'Handsome, classy, tallish, fortyish.'

'You've just described half the women in Vienna. Did you read this?' Holtz demands.

''Course I did. Way things are, you think I want to land up inside?'

Mystified, Holtz quotes from the note, 'The Palace of Whims? A spotted mask! Is this a hoax?'

'In my experience people don't fork out ten ducats for a hoax. I've stayed here too long,' says the man, looking around shiftily before running off into the growing darkness, leaving Holtz to study the note again, undecided.

SIXTEEN

The Masked Woman

*I*N THE PALACE of Whims, which could be considered Vienna's most exclusive nightclub, masked spectators toy with their exotic drinks, flirt and watch in a desultory sort of way the dancing silhouettes of a Chinese shadow play.

A masked woman in a satin cape and hood intercepts a rather lost-looking Holtz, self-conscious in a dog mask.

'Herr Holtz?'

Despite his preparedness he is confused and can only nod a reply.

'I was fearful you might not appear,' she confides.

Holtz collects himself. 'That *was* my inclination.'

'Please believe me, I would have subjected neither of us to this masquerade had I not desperately needed your help.'

'I came out of curiosity,' Holtz admits, 'but if it concerns Beethoven I will most certainly hear you out.'

'It concerns the Immortal Beloved,' comes the staggering reply.

Holtz blinks in amazement. Can this be the Immortal Beloved herself? Who else but she could know of a document locked away, for who knows how many years, in Beethoven's secret drawer? Without another word the masked woman turns and makes her way through the crowd.

Fearful of losing her in the semi-darkness, Holtz sticks close to her heels and only pauses for the briefest moment when she sweeps aside the curtains of a private booth and, with a meaningful look, invites him to enter.

The interior is a kitsch rose bower of paper flowers with a divan of artificial petals, a cupid holding a tray with glasses and a bottle of white wine in a bucket of ice. The masked woman catches sight of Holtz's raised eyebrows.

'This was the most demure booth available.' Without ceremony she pours them both a drink and signals for Holtz to be seated. 'So you've found the letters.'

'There are a great many letters from all sorts,' replies Holtz, hedging.

'Where were they hidden?' she asks, overriding him. 'Ludwig said he could never remember.'

'I would like to know whom I'm addressing,' says Holtz evenly.

The masked woman sits beside him. 'I am a friend of the Immortal Beloved. The letters will be auctioned, of course?'

Holtz nods. 'May I ask why you are so concerned for your friend?'

'Isn't it perfectly obvious?' she says with a hint of impatience.

Holtz hazards a guess. 'Fear of scandal, I suppose – presuming she's a married woman.'

'I would like to make you a pre-sale offer. I'm sure you have no desire to drag some poor middle-aged lady's name through the mud.'

'I am not a scandalmonger, madame, but at the same time the truth must be served,' responds Holtz with a touch of pomposity.

'So you will not part with the letters,' she says, her voice hardening.

'You may bid for them at auction,' Holtz replies curtly.

'After they've become common knowledge.'

Holtz abruptly gets up. 'I regret I cannot assist you.'

The masked woman also stands. 'May I ask one more question?'

'Of course,' says Holtz, politely.

'Who is she, do you think?'

Holtz adopts a hint of melodrama. 'I believe I am speaking to her now. You, Madame Bettina von Arnim, are the Immortal Beloved.'

As she sinks back on to the divan it is clear the masked woman is visibly shaken. She cannot disguise the tremor in her voice. 'And may I ask how you arrived at this fantastic conclusion?'

'With respect, you are not a great actress, madame,' Holtz says drily. 'As to your identity, I deduced that by a process of elimination and a careful perusal of the letters.' He is clearly warming to his theory. 'The first important fact I had to establish was when they were written. They were dated Monday 6 July and Tuesday 7 July – of the year there was no mention.'

'And there must have been many times during his lifetime when 6 and 7 July fell on those days of the week,' the woman interjects.

'Exactly,' says Holtz. 'There was a Monday 6 July in 1789, then again in

1795 – too young to use the phrase "At my age I now need stability". The next time they coincided was 1801, when he was in love with Guicciardi. She wasn't married at the time, and I'm convinced the Immortal Beloved was. The letter is a cry of despair from a man who knows this is his last chance of finding true love – and Giulietta was only the first of many. Next comes 1807, when he was in Baden, and the letter wasn't written there.'

'How do you know?' she demands.

'I'll come to that later,' says Holtz in full flight. 'Neither was it written in Vienna where he spent the entire summer of 1818 – the *last* time the date fits.'

'By simple arithmetic you've omitted a year,' observes the woman.

'Ah, yes: 1812. From his letter it's clear he's taking the waters at a spa,' says Holtz triumphantly. 'In 1812 Beethoven spent the early part of July at Teplitz. The Beloved was staying at a place referred to as "K", which was close enough for a direct mail service by coach. That must have been Karlsbad, correct?' The masked woman is still as a statue. 'In 1812 you had been married less than a year to the young poet Achim von Arnim. He was handsome, talented and a good deal younger than Beethoven, whom you rejected in his favour. It may be presumptuous of me, but dare I suggest that you soon realized you had chosen the wrong man and set about putting the matter right?'

The masked woman seems about to faint. Holtz is alarmed. She removes her mask, revealing features of great beauty.

'You simplify to the point of brutality, sir. I loved my husband very much. I still do.'

'Of course. I merely meant to suggest that you realized too late that you loved Beethoven more. I'm sorry, are you all right?'

'A little cold water, if you please.'

Holtz looks around him for a moment, spies her wine glass, throws away the contents, dips it into the ice bucket and hands it back brimming over. Bettina takes a couple of sips, then holds the glass against her forehead. Holtz is relieved to see that she is regaining her self-control.

'Where were the letters hidden?' she asks again. 'Dear God, I wish I'd never returned them to him! He said he could never remember where he'd put them.'

'They were locked away in a secret drawer.'

Bettina, somewhat reassured by his sympathetic attitude, becomes more trusting. 'He was a wild man, but he could be very tender. Do you know his love song "To the Beloved"?' Holtz nods as Bettina goes on to remind him of the meaningful lyrics. '"The tears of your silent eyes with their love-filled splendour. Oh that I might gather them from your cheek before the earth drinks them in . . ." He wrote that for me. It was a Christmas present. The earth – how he loved it. He used to say, "Nature is a glorious school for the heart: the woods, streams and rocks send back the echo of man's desires." That was in the days of peace, of course, before the world became a battleground.'

Holtz listens, enraptured. No more speculation – this is history as it actually happened, from the lips of the Immortal Beloved herself.

But what he will never be privy to are the memories fleetingly flooding her mind even as she speaks. Memories of love-making on a bed of soft green moss and the tender nature music from the second movement of the 'Pastoral' Symphony, which seems to blend them with the landscape so that the very rocks, the wild flowers, flowing streams and swaying trees seem to move in rhythm with their very souls.

Memories of them bathing in a rock pool and Beethoven cupping his hands, pouring water gently over his beloved's brow. And after the baptism the confirmation as Beethoven crowns Bettina with a garland of honeysuckle.

Now the celebration, the dance, stamping, laughing, weaving through a ring of whirling couples, and the 'peasants' merrymaking music' from the 'Pastoral' Symphony. But soon the merrymaking turns to terror with the advent of the storm. Drums thunder, explosions flash, steel rains from the sky; this is a storm of man's making. Beethoven and Bettina scatter with the rest and run off through the trees to escape the onslaught. With such vivid memories she feels compelled to give voice to, Holtz listens entranced.

'The French bombardment was more terrible than you can imagine. The very earth seemed to erupt. The city was in flames. We sought refuge at the house of my brother Franz. Well, really it was the home of his wife Toni. She'd just inherited it from her father. I remember we all sat in the cellar among his artworks. And as the explosions grew nearer, so did our fear grow, too. Beethoven alone displayed courage as he cried out in defiance, "If I were a general and knew as much about strategy as I know about music I'd teach that bastard a lesson." Then snatching up a cane he wielded it like a sabre and even as he conducted sang the irresistible finale of the Fifth Symphony. You could almost see his cane carving a fiery path through the air, igniting flags, melting cannons, till by the final stabbing chords the enemy has faded away, and, like one possessed, Beethoven leaned against the wall, panting. I tell you I think we were more shattered by Beethoven than the bombardment.'

Holtz listens to Bettina as she continues reminiscing. 'He wove a spell around me with his music. I once asked him the meaning of a certain piano piece, I think it was the Appassionata. "Read *The Tempest*," he growled. From then on I always saw us as Prospero and Miranda. So when he proposed . . .' she hesitates.

Holtz surmises, 'You turned him down.'

'Well, you can't very well marry your father, can you?'

'Fifteen years' difference isn't so much.'

'I realized that as soon as I married Achim.'

'The letter suggests you were ready to sacrifice that marriage for Beethoven.'

'I nearly did – but it would have been too cruel.' Realizing she has said too much Bettina decides it is time to part. 'Should you change your mind about the letters, here is my card. I hope we shall meet again.' For the first time, tears well in her eyes.

Holtz, feeling rather ashamed, takes the card.

'Do you mind leaving me now?' she says quietly. 'I would like to stay here for a while, alone.'

Holtz jumps to his feet. 'Of course, forgive me. It's . . .' He grabs her hand and, overcome with emotion, kisses it. 'It's just . . . I'm overwhelmed . . . to have actually met you.'

Bettina gives way to tears and lowers her head, sobbing. Holtz hesitates no longer and with a stiff little bow is gone. For a few moments Bettina continues to cry, then, blowing her nose, sniffs and indulges in a wicked, self-satisfied little smile. Bitch!

SEVENTEEN

The Coded Message

WHEN HOLTZ RETURNS to Beethoven's lodging less than an hour later he finds the place swept, scrubbed and tidy. In the glow of an oil lamp Fanny has laid out Beethoven. She is writing in her diary. There is a small bunch of flowers near by. Of Schindler there is no sign.

'Evening, Fanny. Where's the watchdog gone?'

'Gone out to chew on a bone, I expect.'

'My God, Fanny, you can actually move about without treading on a symphony. How you do it all *and* keep up a diary is beyond me.'

Fanny pauses in her writing and looks sadly at Beethoven. 'What have they done to him? I've kept this diary ever since he came to the school on that first day with Karlie.'

'Keep it a secret diary. Don't ever air it to the world, Fanny,' says Holtz sadly. 'You may betray more of yourself than him.'

'A 37-year-old spinster, you mean,' says Fanny bitterly. 'I shall never publish it! Schindler left you a message on the bureau.'

Holtz turns to the bureau, expecting to see a sheet of paper, but there is no sign of one. 'Your zeal has exceeded itself. There's no note here.'

'I didn't say "note", I said "message". The cribbage board. He said you'd understand.'

Frowning, Holtz examines the cribbage board, which has a round ivory peg stuck in one of the holes. Holtz removes it and picks up two playing cards near by – the eight and two of hearts – and chuckles.

'Well I never, he's playing a game with me. Now it's my turn to deal.' He shuffles through the remaining pack.

'I wouldn't have thought this was the right moment for games,' remarks Fanny.

'You're wrong there,' says Holtz, laughing. '*He* would have approved. And I play the joker.' He throws the card down in triumph.

She looks at him with concern. 'Are you all right? You haven't been drinking or anything?'

'I have, my dear Fanny. I have been carousing with none other than the Immortal Beloved. Not that she means anything to you. Perhaps I should explain –'

'Save your breath. I've had enough of her for one night, thank you very much.'

Now it is Holtz's turn to pay attention, as she attempts to resume her writing. 'Has Schindler been talking?'

'On and on about it, until I told him who she really was. That silenced him.'

'I'm not surprised,' says Holtz, though he is.

'I am,' scoffs Fanny. 'That you didn't think of her before, I mean.'

'What?' asks Holtz, blinking.

'Well, you were talking to her yourself in this very room only last year.' Fanny sees Holtz is baffled. 'We do have the same lady in mind, I suppose.'

'The woman I met an hour ago was a stranger to me.'

'Then you got the wrong one,' laughs Fanny. 'I've known about her for years, ever since Karlie was a pupil at Daddy's school. Beethoven used to wear a gold wedding ring to remind him of his beloved – his "distant beloved" he called her. He never confessed her name, but he could never get her out of his mind.'

Holtz is stunned. 'But *you* guessed her identity.'

'Only last year, but I'm not telling. I promised Schindler I wouldn't. He left you a clue, though.'

Holtz, totally confused, returns to the bureau and examines the two cards left by Schindler.

'The eight and two of hearts?' He looks at her questioningly.

'I'll give you one clue,' she says tantalizingly. 'The only clue Beethoven ever gave me. He dedicated one of his pieces to her.'

Holtz looks up from the cards in triumph. 'It's an opus number: eighty-two. Let me see . . . Opus 82 was Five Italian Songs, 1809. Damn! No dedication.' Fanny smiles, shakes her head. 'Ah, then it's Opus 28,' says Holtz brightly. 'Yes, Sonata in D major – the "Pastoral".' His face falls. 'Dedicated to *Joseph* von Sonnenfels.' He looks at Fanny aghast. She laughs more than ever.

He throws the cards down in a rage and immediately hits upon the solution. 'Eureka! The Hammerklavier! *Sonata* No. 28, dedicated to . . . no, it can't be her.'

She gives a nod of affirmation. 'I'd have told you anyway.'

'It's just not possible,' exclaims Holtz. 'Why, I was talking to her myself only . . .'

Fanny smiles and returns to her diary as Holtz remembers a day of utter chaos some time in July only last year – the significance of which he was completely unaware at the time.

EIGHTEEN

The Masked Man

BEETHOVEN IS SLUMPED in a chair, half dressed, with the mask-maker Danhauser and assistant Tantfl both stirring plaster like mad. Schindler at work on his biography is like an annoying gnat with his questions and poised pencil, while Fanny bustles about searching for something, all to badly played piano music in the next room.

'And I crap every morning at 8 a.m. sharp,' yells Beethoven. 'Don't leave that out of your damn biography! "Beethoven as I Knew Him" – hah!'

Danhauser begins to slap on plaster as Beethoven shouts at the heavy-handed pianist in the next room.

'God in heaven, boy! Keep time. You've fingers like a bunch of bananas. Yaagh! Danhauser, where's the straws? I can't breathe, man!'

'The Fifth, Master,' says Schindler. 'What was the inspiration for the opening?'

'I'm not a corpse, man,' yells Beethoven, as plaster covers his nose. 'I need air.'

'One moment, Master,' says Danhauser, near panic. 'Hold his arms, Tantfl!'

Danhauser inserts straws up Beethoven's nostrils while Tantfl pins him in the chair.

Schindler persists in his pedantry. 'The opening, Master – was it the yellow-hammer, or Fate knocking on the door?'

'Neither!' jokes Beethoven. 'It was the damned landlord knocking for the rent! Da da dee da! Knock, knock, knock, *knock*, he went.' And as Beethoven gives way to laughter, Danhauser applies a last gob of plaster over his mouth. He nearly chokes.

'Hold still, Master,' urges Danhauser. 'We want to see you as in life – as in life. Hold him still, Tantfl!'

Having looked everywhere with no success Fanny decides to continue her search next door where Beethoven's nephew, Karlie, continues his inept keyboard exercise watched by his teacher, Holtz, trying unsuccessfully to suppress his laughter.

'I can't do it! It's not funny, Holtz. I hate the damn piano.'

'I wasn't laughing at you, Karlie. It just amazes me how your uncle ever manages to write *anything*. It's like a madhouse in there. He was actually conducting the clock just now. Do you know what he reminded me of when I first met him?'

'No, what?' says Karlie, laughing.

'Robinson Crusoe,' says Holtz. Karlie laughs even harder. 'Move over. Let me play for you,' says Holtz, taking pity on him.

'You're a good fellow, Holtz, but what if he should come in?'

'You'll keep an eye on him, won't you, Fanny?'

But Fanny is preoccupied. 'You haven't seen his new cravat, I suppose?'

'Have you looked on the coat rack?' asks Holtz.

''Course. Very well then.'

And as Fanny keeps an eye on the door, pupil and teacher swap places to good effect, with Karlie taking an occasional peep out of the window down to the street.

Suddenly Fanny sounds the alarm. 'Quick! It's himself!'

Indeed it is. Beethoven's claustrophobia and impatience have triumphed over his vanity. With a great bellow he tears off the plaster and vents his wrath on the unfortunate Fanny peeping through the door.

'Aaaah! Give me air. I can't stand it. Like being buried alive. Have you found that cravat yet?'

By the time Beethoven has entered the room brandishing his ear trumpet, pupil and teacher have resumed their rightful positions with noticeably sad results, seemingly lost on the composer.

'If you're going to shout at me like a servant you can find it yourself,' says Fanny.

Beethoven becomes contrite. 'Forgive me, Fanny. You're the only friend I've got. Have you your fiddle, Holtz? We're expected within the hour.' Before he can reply Beethoven barks at Karlie, 'Keep time, boy!'

In a blind fury Beethoven strides over and slams the lid down on Karlie's fingers. The boy cries out in pain. Holtz and Fanny are shocked into immobility.

'Do you take me for an imbecile?' shouts Beethoven. 'Do you have the faintest idea how I am denying myself to educate you?' He pulls at Karlie's jacket. 'And forking out for this handsome new coat, when mine would have seen me out another two years. What's this?'

A snuff-box falls to the ground. Karlie goes pale.

Beethoven picks it up, examines it, reads the inscription aloud. 'To my darling Karlie, from Mother.' He rounds on the unfortunate Karlie. 'You've been seeing her behind my back, haven't you? *Haven't you?*' No reply. 'Do we have to go back to the confessional at St Mark's? Boy . . . boy, don't you understand? I'm your legal guardian. The courts ruled in my favour. *I'm* your father now . . . I can't, I'm burning to write and I can't . . . Holtz, you will accompany him to and from the polytechnic every day. They can't be trusted; she's trying to steal him back again.'

This is too much for Karlie, who runs from the room in great distress, followed a moment later by Beethoven. A terrible silence descends on the remaining occupants, wretched at the spectacle the great man has made of himself.

In the street outside tears of joy stream down Johanna's face as she hugs her son for dear life. Suddenly an outraged Beethoven appears at the back door with his ear trumpet. Fortunately no one is in the street to witness the event, though faces soon begin to appear at the neighbouring windows. But as the row develops an approaching carriage stops near by.

'The court ruled you were to see the boy but twice a year,' says Beethoven, livid with rage. 'You've usurped the judgement of the law.'

'Fuck the law!' yells Johanna.

'Let him go, d'you hear?' yells Beethoven.

'*You* let him go. The boy needs his mother,' Johanna yells back.

For a moment Johanna's cloak parts and Beethoven sees she is pregnant. 'Mother! Look at you! Whose bastard is that?'

'Watch your tongue. It's a cyst. Just like you to insult a sick woman.'

Beethoven offers his hand to Karlie, who involuntarily cringes away. 'I'm sorry, Karlie.'

Johanna senses something has been going on she should know about. 'He's not been ill-treating you, has he, Karlie?'

Poor Karlie is forced to lie in the hope of peace and quiet. 'No, Mother, of course not.'

'Your hands are all red.'

'The piano lid dropped on them, Mother, when I was playing.'

Johanna takes him by the shoulders. 'On your father's grave – is that the truth? Is it?' Karlie is dumb with fright. His mother shakes him. '*Is* it? If I thought for a minute –'

'Johanna!'

As Johanna capitulates to Beethoven's fierce tone and glowering eye and releases the trembling youth, the outraged composer begins to calm down. 'Come, Karlie, that's enough for today. We must get ready for the soirée.'

Karlie shifts uneasily from foot to foot, an act not lost on his mother.

'He's scared stiff of you. Look at him. He's even too scared to tell you he flunked his exams.'

Karlie freezes like a frightened rabbit.

Beethoven is hurt and disappointed. 'Is that so, Karlie?'

Karlie helplessly nods his head. Beethoven's voice turns to ice. 'Get into the house!'

Karlie kisses his mother and for a moment looks as if he is about to obey Beethoven's command, only to rebel at the last moment. 'I'd like to be alone for a while, Uncle Daddy.'

Beethoven is taken by surprise at this new attitude, shaken, dismayed. 'But we're expected at Count Razumovsky's to hear my new quartet.'

Johanna is about to make another disparaging remark but decides it is more prudent to remain silent. For a moment Karlie wavers, until Beethoven comes to his rescue, his gruff, ungracious manner hiding his true feelings.

'Take yourself off for a walk then! I don't want any dismal spirits hovering around me tonight.'

Numb with unhappiness, Karlie walks off. Johanna's smile of triumph almost incenses Beethoven to violence.

'And if you raise one finger to entice him back into that brothel you call a home I'll set the militia on you.'

But she has the last word. 'Stuff your trumpet up your arse and give us a tune.'

She walks haughtily off in the opposite direction to the path taken by her son. Beethoven, bowed with misery, is about to enter the house when the parked carriage moves towards him. A woman's hand appears through the window and gently touches him on the shoulder. He peers through the carriage window, enraptured, and without a moment's hesitation climbs in and closes the door. A moment later it begins to move off, prompting Fanny, who has witnessed the entire scene from the doorway, to run after it and shout through the window.

'Ludwig – I found it.'

As she throws the cravat inside the carriage she catches sight of an elfish woman in her mid-forties.

Beethoven snatches the cravat and the carriage rumbles off in a cloud of dust.

Fanny watches it until she becomes aware of Holtz standing uncomfortably in the doorway. 'I'm afraid you'll be going to Count Razumovsky's alone.'

'But I can't,' protests Holtz. 'What shall I tell him? What's happening? Who was that?'

'I don't know – a woman; a stranger,' says Fanny, lying.

She brushes past him and enters the house, leaving Holtz to stamp his foot in rage as he watches the mysterious carriage turn a corner and vanish from sight.

NINETEEN

Attempted Suicide

FANNY STANDS BY the prostrate form of Beethoven, spectral in his white shroud, as she finally reveals the identity of the mysterious stranger glimpsed that night back in July.

'It was Dorothea von Ertmann. I thought it imprudent to say so at the time, so I lied to you.'

But Holtz does not wish to give up his Immortal Beloved so easily. 'Sharing a carriage with a lady hardly qualifies her for the love of his life. He admired her, I grant you. She played his music like no other, we all know that, but to suggest –'

'What did you expect?' snaps Fanny. 'A clap of thunder and a heavenly host? A sudden sureness that you are in love with a man is a quiet thing,' she says softly. 'Sometimes it passes unnoticed . . .'

'No, give me proof!' insists Holtz, totally missing the point.

'Patience!' she says calmly. 'Think back. His servant had walked out. The place was in a terrible mess. He became more impossible than ever. He couldn't find anything! His music, money – everyone was stealing from him. For some reason he was obsessed with his diary. It had disappeared. I decided to tidy up one day. I was sweeping under the bed when I caught sight of something. It was a flat-looking wooden case. I opened it and realized it was a duelling box, for two pistols. One was gone. I believe you know the rest.'

'I know Karlie tried to blow his brains out,' says Holtz, before quoting from memory, 'When you have no choice but to live constantly with an inferior person close to you . . .' And then he gives voice to his own thoughts. 'If I ever found out Beethoven had written that about me I'd probably have done the same.'

'I was always telling the old man not to leave that diary around where anyone could find it, but he never would listen to me.'

'Poor boy. One can't but be sorry for him – a failed pianist, a failed suicide.

But what's all that to do with Beethoven and Dorothea von Ertmann?'

'He held himself responsible, and in a sense I suppose he was. He was like a man in a dream. He'd sit over his manuscript paper for hour after hour – didn't write as much as a crochet most of the time, and when he did manage to get down a few notes he'd end up crossing them out and tearing the paper to shreds. And so it went on until the day she came by and started to play for him. It was like a healing balm. You must have sensed that yourself the day you dropped in with the General.'

'How could I forget? She was playing the sonata written specially for her by Beethoven, and you were at the stove stirring something or other in time to the music. I remember thinking, How funny. It *was* funny, don't you think?'

'I suppose it was,' says Fanny flatly.

Then they both fall silent, remembering the incident according to their individual points of view. What actually happened was that the General, a florid, bustling soldier in his early fifties, rudely broke the tranquillity with his momentous news.

'That's settled then,' he declares. 'Von Stutterheim is willing to take the lad into the regiment. Be the making of him!'

Beethoven, very low key, seems to speak his thoughts aloud. 'I wanted him to be free . . . smelling life . . . all the things I couldn't.'

Holtz gently explains, 'Attempted suicide is a criminal offence here in Vienna. By this means we can avoid proceedings . . .'

'No question of it! I assure you,' says the General, turning to his wife. 'Well, er, Dorothea . . . Must wrest you from your beloved pianoforte! Be late for the reception – then, packing, you know. Italy next week.'

'Tried to kill himself rather than be with me,' mumbles Beethoven, shaking his head.

'Nonsense!' says the General forcefully. 'Least thing, et cetera.! For years your music has given us all pleasure. I'm sure Dorothea echoes my sentiments.'

Dorothea rises from the piano regretfully. 'We always leave Vienna with heavy hearts.'

'My sentiments entirely!' says the General earnestly. '*Au revoir*, Maestro. If we are not at war with someone or other by next year we will be sure to visit when we return on our annual furlough.'

'Gave a benefit for the wounded of Hanau once. All those eyes, twisted stumps . . .' muses Beethoven.

'Capital!' exclaims the General uncomprehendingly as he pumps Beethoven's hand, before turning to Holtz with a whisper. 'You sure his ears aren't playing him up? How oddly he replies.' But before Holtz can answer the General takes him to one side. 'A final word. You'd better look to it . . . seeing, er, present state of mind . . . Certain protocol in these matters. Buying a commission takes a certain finesse. Better see Stutterheim yourself. Not much truck with artistic types, you follow me? Not that I'm inferring . . . you understand!'

The remainder of the conversation is lost as they leave the room and clatter downstairs. Beethoven and Dorothea are left alone in the room. The silence between them is profound. Beethoven gently takes her hand. In his eyes there is gratitude and love, and Dorothea's own eyes mirror that love. Fanny comes in with a tureen of soup.

'He must eat. He's had nothing for days.'

Dorothea nods, squeezes Beethoven's hand. 'Please take care of yourself.'

'There's a divinity which shapes our ends, rough hue them how we may. Goodbye.'

A moment later Dorothea has gone. To Beethoven it appears that the breath of life has also gone. He allows Fanny to seat him at the table, even to put the spoon in his hand. With a pinched little smile she encourages him to eat. To please her, he takes a sip of gruel. Then laying down the spoon, he rises from the table.

'Tired. Finish it later.'

He lies down on the bed as still as death, and indeed the will to live has gone out of him. Fanny watches him, a tear trickling down her cheek.

TWENTY

Bone of Contention

As she stands in the same spot looking at the dead Beethoven lying on the bed, her features show the same compassion.

Holtz breaks the spell. 'Touching, I'll grant you. But nothing you've said constitutes proof.'

Fanny is disillusioned. 'Taken all in all, there's not much to choose between you and Herr Schindler! You weren't there all the time. I knew, I tell you.'

'Since we're being so forthright,' replies Holtz grimly, 'admit a dose of jealousy in your character. No, it's not good enough. Because she played the piano well! They could all play the piano!'

'Including your prime choice!' she scoffs. 'Ha!'

Holtz is caught off guard. 'Bettina can play . . .'

She is amazed. 'You can't be serious!' She sees he is and continues with derision. 'Oh, certainly. She can play all right. Her improvisations are legendary! That woman is making a career out of being the "inspiration" of every great man from Goethe to Beethoven. If he'd been a contemporary she'd claim to have set Shakespeare afire, too. You're stupid, Herr Holtz. Can't you see it? What a coup if she were the recipient of the greatest love letters of the age. If she could only claim that! The lady has made an art out of her vicarious pleasures. You think he didn't know she hung on every word and reported it to the newspapers before the spittle was dry on his lips?'

Holtz is incredulous. 'Brand herself an adulteress? Never!'

'Her husband was going to be the greatest poet of the century. All he's done is plagiarize other works. Bit of a come-down for someone who was going to be the second Goethe. A little notoriety would be the making of the pair of them. What she couldn't exaggerate, she made up. She followed Ludwig around like a parasite. I thought you had more integrity, Herr Holtz, really I did.'

He rallies. 'Then tell me how she knew of those Immortal Beloved letters? Are you suggesting Dorothea von Ertmann would confide such a titbit to your scandalmonger?'

She stops in her tracks. To her this seems unlikely; however, she is reluctant to concede to Holtz. 'Perhaps they're in league. Who knows? Perhaps Dorothea is not all saint – God knows, he wasn't! But I'll guarantee this, mark my words: Before the year is out Madame Bettina will mysteriously "discover" a dozen more love letters, and the publishers will be tripping over themselves to get at them before the ink's dry.'

'Preposterous!'

'Preposterous yourself!' she fires back, seething. 'To think such a little sycophant could ever get near that man. As if he would ever explain himself to her!'

She drops to her knees at Beethoven's bedside and gives way to tears. At this moment Schindler enters the room, breathless and excited. Some of his elation dissipates at the sight of Fanny and Holtz.

'Have you two been fighting at a time like this? You disgust me.'

Fanny quickly rises to her feet and blows her nose. 'The two of you put together don't come near to a man! Like dogs around a carcass. You think more of your damned Immortal Beloved than you do of him . . . of the loss! Go away and leave the poor man in peace.'

'You don't understand,' says Holtz. 'I have to know. It's important to understand.'

Schindler cuts in, 'How can you say that? My regard for the Maestro knew no bounds.'

Fanny simply goes to the door, open it and waits for them to leave. After a moment's hesitation they do so. Fanny closes the door after them and leans back against it, utterly drained.

TWENTY-ONE

Reluctant Allies

H OLTZ AND SCHINDLER are standing face to face in the street below. An uneasy alliance has sprung up between them.

'I hope your proof has more substance than hers,' says Holtz, 'because I must tell you that tonight I came face to face with the Immortal Beloved herself.'

'You saw Dorothea von Ertmann – here, in Vienna?' asks Schindler incredulously.

'The Immortal Beloved is *not* von Ertmann!'

'But I have irrefutable proof.'

'If it is as flimsy as hers, heaven help us!'

'I tell you I have proof!' says Schindler, raising his voice. 'Written proof! And what is more –'

He is interrupted by the sound of a window opening. Fanny is looking down at them. She hurls out Holtz's coat, which in his haste he forgot, and quickly closes the window.

'I need a drink. There's a Bierhaus around the corner,' he says, picking up his coat and dusting it off.

To his surprise Schindler catches his arm. 'No. *He* used to go there. For tonight, let us go somewhere that has no hint of the past about it. The Chocolate Soldier.'

Holtz grins. 'It's for sure he never went there!'

He falls in step with Schindler as they walk off together into the darkness, laughing.

The Chocolate Soldier is a respectable coffee-house with clientele as sober as its décor. Half a dozen couples chat discreetly, partaking of snacks and drinks.

Schindler and Holtz sip hot chocolate and nibble at brandy snaps. They still don't trust each other – for the time being at least.

'We could speculate endlessly on the women in Beethoven's life and their personal involvement with him,' says Schindler, 'but unless they were at Karlsbad on 6 July, fifteen years ago precisely, they could never qualify as the Immortal Beloved.'

'Granted,' says Holtz. 'Tell me something I don't know.'

'If I show you proof – irrefutable proof – will you give me your word that you will never publish it?'

'How many times do I have to tell you?' says Holtz, close to exasperation. 'I am not interested in publication, but in understanding the *man* ... for myself. I give you my word. Anyway, why share it with me if it's so controversial?'

'Because I have an overriding desire to see you beaten, my friend,' says Schindler with obvious contempt. 'May I be frank? He never liked me, and he made me know it. Now I want to see *your* face.'

'That's honest enough,' says Holtz with a smile. 'And if it's of any relevance, I never liked you either. This is pointless. I swear that I shall never link the name of Dorothea von Ertmann with the Master's love letters. Does that satisfy you?'

Satisfied, Schindler take a folded newspaper from an inside pocket and gives it to Holtz, who unfolds it.

'The *Karlsbad Journal*, Wednesday 8 July 1812 . . . where should I be looking?'

'Page five, second column,' says Schindler. 'More chocolate?'

'Not for me – tastes like weak cow slurry.' Holtz scans the paper. 'The Social Register? What of it?'

'Dear Holtz, you must curb your desire to imitate him. It doesn't sit well. The Social Register – a list of every visitor to Karlsbad in the week in question. Personally I find the chocolate excellent – the sweet taste of success, perhaps?'

'Every visitor? How could they possibly know every visitor?'

'You've obviously never taken the waters,' says Schindler with a superior smirk. 'It is a veritable parade of worthies. To be left off that list is tantamount to excommunication. Furthermore, it was a troubled time. Everyone had to register with the militia as well – a double indemnity, you might say. Under the Es you'll find Dorothea von Ertmann – the only name on the entire list which can possibly be linked with the Master.'

'Where did you find this?'

'I remembered coming across it when cataloguing my "trivia list", I think you called it. Its significance escaped me at the time, however. And now, my dear Holtz, do you still wish to regale me with *your* mysterious impostor?'

Holtz is disappointed that Schindler has won the day but sees no reason why he should not mention her name. 'I must concede that some evidence of fraud exists, and yet . . .'

He stops, his eyes widen at the sight of another name on the list.

Schindler sees his reaction and is a jump ahead of him. 'Ah-ha! I see you notice it, too. Brentano. Read on. Antonia Brentano and her husband Franz, but Bettina, his sister, wasn't with them. Just as well – two possibilities would have muddied the issue. Now, who is your mysterious lady? A charlatan, as we know, yet she must have been reasonably clever to have taken you in!'

Holtz is suddenly afire. An entirely new possibility has presented itself – one that seems to make total sense at last. Bettina borrowed the letters from her sister-in-law – not von Ertmann, therefore . . . On no account will he volunteer this information to Schindler. Instead he lays a smoke-screen. 'You have me. I capitulate. I'm embarrassed. I most humbly congratulate you on your perspicacity. Suddenly today has caught up with me, and I feel immeasurably tired. I must get some sleep before the "big event".'

'A rather ghoulish flippancy, if I may say so. Everything should run smoothly.'

'They've readied the burial plot?' asks Holtz, not wishing to appear too eager to be off.

'Nice spot, shielded from the weather. Not too exposed to the sky. Grillparzer has prepared a magnificent oration for the ceremony. I'd like to hear what you think . . .' From another pocket he fishes a scrap of paper from which he drones, '"He fled the world because he could not find in the whole compass of his loving nature a weapon with which to resist it. He withdrew from his fellow men after he had given them everything and had received nothing in return. He remained alone because he found no second self. But until his death, he preserved a human heart for his own people, the whole world . . ."' He trails off, aware that Holtz is not listening. 'Et cetera. Rather moving, I felt.'

'You might have written it yourself. Goodnight,' says Holtz, leaping to his feet and rushing out.

Schindler puts Holtz's rude departure down to disappointment or drink or both. Smiling complacently, he dunks a biscuit as he pulls out some publisher's proofs and corrects them on the table before him.

Somewhat the worse for drink, Holtz stumbles along a dimly lit side street with glee.

He's cracked it!

TWENTY-TWO

Nemesis

O UTSIDE A PICTURESQUE but neglected one-storey building, made romantic by the moonlight, Holtz checks the number on a piece of paper. Straightening his cravat he knocks at the door. Receiving no response he knocks again – harder. Moments later a sleepy manservant in a nightshirt opens the door a crack and peeps cautiously out.

'Yes?'

'I must see Madame von Arnim immediately. She **is** expecting me,' Holtz lies.

'My Lady is abed. What name shall I say?'

Holtz roars, 'Nemesis!'

The manservant is unconcerned. 'If you will be good enough to wait, sir.'

Holtz, enjoying himself immensely, shouts, 'Tell her it's Fate knocking at her door.'

Moments later the lady of the house appears and with a smile invites him in. 'I knew you would come.' She turns to the servant. ' Prepare the drawing-room, Hans.'

Hans shuffles off, muttering. Bettina turns to Holtz, still smiling. 'You see, I knew that your natural benevolence would prevail. Please . . .'

To his surprise, she takes him by the arm and leads him along the passage.

In the drawing-room the glow from the fire Hans is rekindling throws a kindly light on the furnishings, which have seen better days. As Hans takes his leave Bettina seats herself on a rug in front of the fire and smiles up at Holtz as he stands uneasily near by.

In the soft, flattering light she looks years younger – and knows it. 'Do be at ease,' she croons. 'What prompted you finally?'

'I wanted to see the Immortal Beloved,' says Holtz boldly.

'You are flattering me,' says Bettina, flirtatiously. 'Once was surely enough? You know, I *must* have those letters. They are mine by right. Now we have to only discuss the price.'

'That is a matter for your sister-in-law, surely,' says Holtz.

Bettina goes pale but otherwise hides her distress. 'Antonia? What has she got to do with this?'

'You insulted my intelligence once, madame. Don't attempt it again,' says Holtz with growing candour.

Bettina guesses Holtz has seen through her deception and decides to abandon the seductress in favour of the martyr. 'I'm glad it is out! You cannot imagine the burden of living a lie! But I love her so much!'

'Evidently, madame. Where can I find her?'

'You must understand that I act as intermediary.'

Holtz feels insulted. 'Do I look like a blackmailer?'

'Of course not, but any personal contact . . . the scandal – husband, children.' She crawls across to Holtz and places her arms on the chair, pinning him in. 'Is there nothing I can do to dissuade you? Nothing . . . at all?'

Holtz gets up, suddenly sickened. 'Madame, you have no dignity.'

As he strides out of the room, she runs after him. She catches him at the doorway and flings her arms around his neck.

'Please! Let me have the letters – I beg of you.'

Holtz is sickened by her duplicity. 'Goodnight, madame!' He tears himself from her embrace and throws open the door.

Facing him is a veiled woman in black.

Bettina is even more staggered than he is.

Before they can collect themselves the woman in mourning speaks. 'Dear Bettina!' she exclaims with a sigh. 'How reassuring. You never change! I spend my entire life colliding with your respective amours. Young man, are you going in or coming out? You may be perfectly frank, I assure you I am quite the woman of the world!' She turns to address the driver of the carriage, who is walking in with her bags. He also carries a huge wreath of wild flowers. 'First floor, third door on the left.' To Bettina, 'I take it that *is* still the guest room, my dear?'

Bettina nods.

The woman resumes giving order to the coachman. 'Be here at noon, and remember – I want full dressage on the horses, plumes, everything, and ribbons on the cortège.'

'I know the very best undertaker, madame. It shall be done.' The coach-man bows his way upstairs with the luggage, leaving the woman to take command.

'Well, are we going to deliberate on the doorstep all night or go in. I'm freezing!' And before anyone can protest she is sweeping them back into the drawing-room.

Holtz cannot hide his excitement. Here at last is the Immortal Beloved herself – Toni Brentano. Bettina capitulates as Toni continues to take the initiative.

'Brandy, Bettina! That carriage is cold enough to serve as the hearse itself! Does your young man ride with you tomorrow? No lilies, young man. Take a tip – *wild* flowers if you don't want to risk eternal damnation!'

Uncharacteristically, Holtz finds himself tongued-tied.

'I'm sorry, Antonia, I had no idea you were coming,' says Bettina apolo-getically.

'No apology necessary, my dear, but did you imagine I would neglect to see him on his way? I must bid him *bon voyage*, I simply must.'

'Is Franz not with you?' asks Bettina, still all at sea.

'Oh, you've finally noticed,' says Antonia. 'He's away on business.'

'This, er, young man is also here on business of a kind,' says Bettina, hoping her sister-in-law will not get the wrong impression.

Holtz blushes, too deeply embarrassed to speak.

Bettina finally blurts it out, 'He found the letters.' She lets out a sigh of relief and gives a glass of brandy to Toni.

She knocks it back in a couple of gulps and finally says, 'Letters? What letters?'

Having nearly reached boiling point, Holtz finds his voice. 'The love letter to the Immortal Beloved. He wrote them to you in the summer of 1812.'

'Oh, 1812 . . . *Those* letters! You mean Ludwig.' Holtz is as stunned by her casual attitude as he is by her explanation. 'Ludwig's grasp of the finer points of our language was a little vague – and he spoke rough German, you understand – actually he meant "Eternal", not "Immortal". There's a subtle difference.' She gives a long yawn. 'They've always meant more to Bettina than they did to me, didn't they, dearest? I should never have told you about them. You've done nothing but stew over them ever since. One would think the universe revolved around them! And, darling, my glass is empty.'

She takes another brandy from a crushed Bettina and sips it thoughtfully and shrewdly.

Holtz is staggered.

'Oh dear,' exclaims Toni. 'By the look of you, young man, it would appear there has been some major catastrophe in your particular universe, too.'

'I am one of Beethoven's executors,' says Holtz reverently.

'So. And what do you intend to do with the letters?' Antonia asks casually.

'I'm afraid they must be disposed of with the rest of his estate. An auction seems likely,' says Holtz. 'To return them to you would only excite curiosity – they have already been catalogued, you see, and copies exist. All kinds of speculation would ensue if the originals went missing. But I can assure you as a man of honour, madame, that no one will learn about them from me – least of all your husband!'

'My dear young man, what are you talking about? My husband read those letters years ago. He knew of our love. That is why I immediately knew it must end. That is why I gave them back to Ludwig. He was quite relieved. You see, I might so easily have blown him off course . . . You look puzzled, Herr Holtz. This is obviously not how you pictured the dénouement, is it? Are you a musician?'

'Yes, madame,' says Holtz proudly. 'The violin.'

Antonia replies softly, 'No. There is a world of difference between a musician and a fiddler. Ludwig was an artist, bestowed with some extraordinary insight by which to manifest what is divine. Oh, he loved me all right. Wanted me, and because I loved him it had to end. I'll tell you *why* he loved me. I think I was the only person who acknowledged his fate, and I never tried to steer him away from it. And it doesn't matter a damn if they find out about me or don't. Poor young man, the bottom has quite dropped out of your theory, hasn't it? Find the lady, find the *man*? Thereby to be handed Beethoven's *raison d'être* upon a plate! How unfortunate – you are back on your own! Never mind. You're but the first of many. I see successive generations or prospectors all digging for gold, all trying to quantify "the maverick". You'll think of some-thing. Isn't that so, Bettina?' Bettina lowers her eyes, caught out. 'You say you are his executor. Why not accept his wonderful legacy and thank God you have ears to hear it?'

'You want . . . nothing?' asks Holtz in amazement.

'Only the last thing he ever wrote. What was it? Positively the *last* thing. Do you know?'

Holtz fishes in his pocket and takes out a scrap of paper. 'I found it by the bed. It's just a scrawl. I was going to throw it away. It's not music . . .'

'Read it to me,' she says simply.

Holtz hesitates, takes a deep breath and says, 'That's it. That's the lot . . .' Antonia roars with laughter, leaving Holtz completely perplexed. 'I can understand why he loved you, madame – I say this with deep humility – but I cannot understand why you seem so . . . so . . .'

Antonia finishes for him, 'Elated? You cannot have read the letters very closely. Florid text, as I said. Ludwig could never overcome his clumsy language, but even in 1812 he had some grasp of what eternity means. Schiller said it so much better. I remember that last time. My husband Franz was there, and the children. We were in the hills above Karlsbad. Ludwig was practically busting with joy, shouting Schiller's poem to the skies. He wanted to set it to music – it had been gnawing at him since he was a boy. That day it was as if he had finally captured something.' And much to the surprise of both Holtz and Bettina, Antonia begins to sing:

> Oh friends, let's not be mournful,
> Let us sing a happy song, and joyful.
>
> Joy you gleaming spark divine
> Daughter of Elysium.
> Drunk with fire we draw near
> Immortal Goddess to thy holy shrine.
>
> Your magic unites again
> What habit has forced apart.
> All mankind shall be
> Brother beneath your spreading wing.
>
> He whose good fortune grants him
> Friends to have and friend to be;
> Who has won a noble woman
> Let him join in our rejoicing.
> Yes – were there one heart only
> Beating for him in the world.

Antonia's enthusiasm is infectious, and both Holtz and Bettina feel compelled to join in, even though vocally far from perfect.

> All creatures drink joy
> At nature's breast,
> Good and bad alike
> Follow her rosy path.
>
> Kisses she gave us and the vine,
> A trusty friend unto death.
>
> Glad as his suns that speed
> Through the spaces of heaven
> Brothers, run your course
> Joyful as a hero in victory.
> Be embraced, you millions!
> For the universe this kiss!
> Brothers, above the canopy of stars
> A loving father surely dwells.
> Fall to your knees, you millions.
> Do you sense the creator of the world?
> Seek him above the starry heavens.
> Surely he dwells above the stars.

By the time the song reaches its climax, led by Antonia, they have gravitated to the window and are looking out into the night, occupied with their own thoughts.

It is Antonia who finally breaks the silence. 'We shall surely meet above the stars.'

And as all three continue to contemplate the wonder of the firmament, Beethoven's transcendental realization of Schiller's poem begins to fill their consciousness, continually growing in splendour until the entire universe seems to be singing Beethoven's symphony.

'That's it.

'That's the lot . . .'

Brahms Gets Laid

Contents

BRAHMS GETS LAID

Prologue

S HE CAME AT him out of the mist. Perhaps that is why he did not recognize her at first. And, though he had known her for nigh on half a century and lusted after her on more than one occasion, he had never seen her naked before. Not even in his wildest dreams.

Her bright hair was loose, as he had not seen it for years. A slight breeze lifted strands of it, as though spinning a gossamer cloak off her bare shoulders. Her breasts made him weep with loneliness and desire.

With a reassuring smile, she embraced him; and without further ado she effortlessly bore him aloft, carpet-bag and all. He was in heaven. The touch of her embrace was like a sustained B sharp that teased his answering blood into an ecstatic pitch.

Up through the clouds they soared and ever onward, over the mountains towards black – the black, black forest with its pine tops scraping the blue ice bowl of the sky. He knew that forest, didn't he? Where something was nailed to a tree. To the very tallest tree. Something that, as they descended, began to resemble – oh, no – a pair of human testicles. Full of human seed.

Now he and she were circling above a grand piano in a clearing. A pretty, petite woman was at the keyboard, her lace-like hands confidently tracing patterns of caress on the ivories. He blew her a kiss, to which she did not respond.

As she continued to play, the cascading notes turned into clouds of butter-flies, orange monarchs and indigo flimtails and sweet cabbage whites, which the seven children dancing around her tried to capture in big black nets.

That was when he recognized them all.

The figure at the keyboard was none other than Snow White. And the seven cavorting figures were the seven dwarves. This startling revelation sickened him, like a secret he was sworn to defend against probable assault.

Suddenly two men in butchers' aprons appeared, leading a lamb on a rope. When they arrived at the grand piano with its raised lid, they held the struggling animal above the exposed vibrating strings and slit the lamb in two. Mucus and organs spilled from its wound. Gradually the piano filled with blood.

But nobody paid any attention, not even when a handsome prince galloped up on a fine black stallion, stripped off and climbed into the piano of blood. The prince began to sing in a foreign language he did not comprehend.

In any case, everything was getting smaller as they sped onward in their flight, towards a big city where in the main square a naked baby with a big erection was banging away on a baby grand piano. Painted women in *déshabillé* danced with carnival figures in animal masks and claws, while the burghers of the city – all in blindfolds – turned their backs on the spectacle and put their fingers in their ears.

Up, up and away again to another city. Down, down, down towards the ornate domes and towers blooming into view. Towards the golden statues of heroes standing guard on imperial rooftops. Squares of green lay scattered far below like bits of broken chessboard. Rows of teacake houses with chocolate trim swam before his eyes. He was feeling a little dizzy. Was it the journey or the lack of food?

Ouch! That landing on a park bench had been rather hard. He opened his eyes, wrestling to sit upright. His dream girl had gone. Only the sound of his own gasping breath greeted him.

Then he realized. It was the iron park bench itself that was hard. He had been sleeping on it all night and was stiff with cold.

He got to his feet, stretching his limbs in the morning sun. He ran around the bench a couple of times to restore circulation, picked up his carpet-bag and set off on a brisk ten-minute walk that was to change his life.

As he did so, he tried to remember the dream in detail. How weird. Was it a prophecy or a memory?

He would analyse it later.

ONE

A Stranger in Town

CLUTCHING HIS CARPET-BAG he looked about him with furtive glances as he walked slowly past one of the most impressive houses on a street of impressive houses.

Was he loitering with intent? No, he was too well dressed to be a thief, unless it were a gentleman thief – and yet he wore no top hat, as was the custom, which marked him out as a little, well, if not exactly odd then somewhat unconventional. No, he was not a felon; he was simply trying to summon up the courage to mount the steps and knock on the big front door, hoping to be greeted by one of the stars he so much admired. He preferred that it would be Robert, but he would almost be as happy to be greeted by his glamorous wife Clara.

A sudden thought stopped him dead in his tracks as he dived a hand into his pocket to see if 'it' was still there. Instant relief! It was: a glowing letter of introduction assuring Mr and Mrs Schumann that the bearer, Johannes Brahms, was a young composer on the threshold of genius, more than worthy of their attention. And it was signed Joseph Joachim, a personal friend of theirs who just happened to be the greatest living violinist on the planet – or so thought his best pal Brahms.

So why hesitate?

Just bound up those steps, Joe, he said to himself, and give that brass knocker the old Beethoven 5 treatment, the old Rat-tat-tat-TAAT! Rat-tat-tat-TAAT! Symbol of courage and victory!

Instead he crept around the side and knocked on the back door like an apologetic hobo hoping for a hand-out.

His timid knock was answered by a harassed, buxom servant holding a two-year-old girl. Behind them was a group of busy children beating rhythmically on the kitchen table with spoons and belting out a popular song of the day . . .

The mice crawled up the cupboard
They thought it rather nice
The mice crawled up the cupboard
And ate up all the rice.

. . . which they repeated over and over. Brahms panicked and retreated without uttering a single word. He had got the wrong address, obviously. This must be an orphanage. No, wait a minute, hadn't his mate Joachim said something about the Schumann glee club? Maybe he wasn't joking, and this was it.

By now Brahms was about to fly out the front gate, when he happened to collide with the handsome couple coming in. Brahms was nonplussed. How he wished he'd had a hat. It would have given him something to do with his hands, as he panicked and turned red with embarrassment. He could have tipped it, fiddled with it, anything to have stopped those big hands fluttering about like oversized cabbage white butterflies.

'*Papillons*,' the couple said simultaneously, breaking into laughter, whereupon something burst through Brahms's shy barrier, enabling him to burst into song. Now it was the Schumanns' turn to be astonished as they recognized No. 5 of Robert's Butterfly Studies, perfectly transposed from piano to the human voice. *Wunderbar!* When he finished his vocal fireworks display, both husband and wife applauded ecstatically, as did the five children who had forsaken the meal table to be entranced by this virtuoso pied piper. Little did any of the watchers guess that this was an act of sheer desperation that the shy young man was capable of only at moments of extreme stress.

'Back to your dinner at once,' said 35-year-old Clara, chasing the screaming kids back around the house.

'Mr Johannes Brahms, I presume,' enquired the 46-year-old Robert.

'Yes,' replied Brahms, 'but my friends call me Joe.'

'You're going to be a great hit with the kids, but I really worry that you've made a rod for your own back. At least it will give me a rest from the eternal bedtime stories.'

Brahms grinned. 'Pleased to meet you, Mr Schumann. It's a great honour, I'm sure.'

'Joachim says you like to get sloshed. Let's have a beer,' said Schumann, patting him on the shoulder and walking him up the steps to the big front door.

TWO

Hand Job in Hamburg

'**H**ATS OFF, GENTLEMEN. A genius!' Joe's hair stood up high on the nape of his neck. He knew he was good, but was he really that good? As yet he'd only written a few piano pieces and a handful of songs. He sat back in his armchair, folded the newspaper and continued to read the rave review by his new friend Robert Schumann:

> His name is Johannes Brahms and he comes from Hamburg, where until now he has worked in quiet obscurity. But on the very day of his arrival he sat down at the piano and began to open up regions of wonder, into which Clara and myself were irresistibly drawn.
>
> Add to this a technique of absolute genius, which turns the piano into a magnificent orchestra scintillating with light and colour, and you begin to get the faintest glimmer of his talent. His sonatas are like symphonies and his songs barely need the words to convey their meaning, so clear is their poetic intent.
>
> I predict a brilliant future for the young Johannes, who like his name-sake Johannes the Baptist has come to prophesy the dawning of a new age, a new era in heavenly music, that gives fresh meaning to the word sublime.

Brahms was blushing again. He'd done a lot of blushing lately, after a gap of many years. As a child he had blushed frequently, as most shy little boys would, given the circumstances – the circumstances being getting bounced on the knees of loose women in every whorehouse in Hamburg. But the very familiarity of these actions eventually caused young Joe to become blasé and the blushing to give way to yawns of boredom.

But what was a young lad of ten doing in a brothel in the first place? Well, he was there for the same reason as the tarts – to earn an honest crust. And no one in Hamburg was the equal of Joe Brahms for setting the joint a-jumping when every randy sailor afloat came ashore for his Saturday night shag. And if the occasional mercenary matelot ever needed some incentive, the sight of a lucky little sod getting a gentle hand job usually proved to be an effective turn-on.

From toy boy to triumphant genius in ten years was quite a step, but the fact that he was more skint today than he had been a decade ago was real cause for concern. If it weren't for the generosity of the Schumanns, and their insistence that he take up residence under their roof, he'd be out there sleeping on a park bench.

He sort of paid for his keep by constant baby-sitting. Still, that was no great hardship. They were a great bunch of kids, particularly Marie, whom he quite fancied. All right, so she was just thirteen, but that didn't bother Joe, who wasn't in the least superstitious. What did bother him was the fact that he frequently got the hots for Clara, despite the fact that she had borne seven children, with another on the way. That wasn't a problem. No, the problem was Robert, randy old sod; he couldn't get enough of her, could he? And vice versa, it seemed.

Talk of the Devil – here she was, sweeping briskly into the room as usual, as if there weren't enough hours in the day for all the tasks she had set herself.

Brahms put down his paper and got up.

'Don't get up. Do stay. Robert's going out for a walk so now's my chance to practise, and do I need it! My next recital is only two days off, and it's the Davidsbundler Dances, damn it; and to tell the truth they're a bit of a trial, especially No. 3.' Without ceremony she sat down at the piano and started to play.

Joe broke in, 'Did you say Robert's going for a walk? Think I'll join him. I've just read the article.'

'Good, isn't it?' said Clara. 'That should whet the publishers' appetites. He's already left. You'll have to catch him up.'

'Which direction?'

'The usual. Where else?'

'I'll buy him a drink,' shouted Brahms against a cascade of notes, hurriedly leaving the room as Clara dedicated herself to mastering her husband's music.

THREE

The Blind Cripple

ROBERT WAS JUST about to order when Brahms beat him to it. 'Two of the usual, please, Rudi,' he said to the bewhiskered barman.

But it was Robert who got in the first word to his friend. 'Tell me, are you just glad to see me or has Clara started crucifying that keyboard once again?'

'Meaning?' questioned Brahms.

'Meaning, has her playing driven you out of the house?'

'Not at all. Her playing is sheer heaven, and you know it.'

'Close! She plays like an angel, it's true; but my idea of heaven, absolute heaven, is an eternity of silence. And that's what I need, my friend, if I'm ever to finish my symphony in time for next month's première.'

'Then what on earth are you doing here?' demanded Brahms.

'She's got a very important concert coming up in a couple of days, and Liszt is going to be there, sitting in the front row just waiting for her to fuck up. Need I say more?'

'Do you think he's really that jealous of her?' asked Brahms. 'As king of the keyboard he's unchallenged.'

'Until a queen comes along and knocks him off the throne. Of course, that can only happen if she gets plenty of practice – which out of respect for my needs as a composer she is willing to forgo.'

'So that's why you sacrificed your precious silence. Out of respect for her needs.'

'And it's not just a matter of perfecting her technique,' said Robert. 'She needs time to feel her way into my world.'

'Which is sadly out of reach for most of your regular ivory bashers.'

'So as the family breadwinner she must have priority. My symphonies don't even buy the butter.'

'They will,' reassured Brahms, 'they will. We'll drink to it.'

They raised their glasses.

'And to you, my budding genius,' said Robert.

'I read the article,' said Brahms as they clinked glasses.

'My publishers want to see your sonatas. Let's drink to their success.'

Brahms's face lit up as they clinked their glasses once again and drank up.

As the day progressed they continued to toast one another and became increasingly merry and garrulous. Brahms rambled on about his crazy days spent at the Franz Liszt household in Weimar, into which his great mate Joachim had recently introduced him. Robert reminisced over his nine-year courtship of the teenage Clara while he studied music with her paranoid parent under the same roof, without arousing the slightest suspicion until the day he popped the question – but that's another story.

Things began to change the moment a blind cripple entered, begging for alms. He was a war veteran.

The cripple's effect on Robert was electric. The first thing Brahms noticed was the sweat breaking out on his friend's forehead, then came the trembling, to be followed by a grimace of pain and finally a scream of horror as he put his hands over his ears and ran pell-mell out of the pub.

Everyone was startled, Brahms most of all. It was several seconds before he could recover sufficiently to abandon his beer and run out after Robert full pelt.

FOUR

The 'S' Word

*F*OR A SOMEWHAT flabby forty-something, Schumann could certainly run. But then so could Brahms, who was lithe, fit and fleet of foot. In fact, Brahms soon began to gain on the stressed-out Schumann. The Rhine was in full spate after recent autumn rains as they ran along its banks towards home. *Well, at least he is running in the right direction,* thought Brahms.

But long before the house was in sight Robert took a right on to Ritter's bridge, the one that led directly to the fish market. *Fish market! What's the crazy nut doing making for the fish market? Shit! Now he is climbing up on the superstructure of the bridge. The bugger's about to jump!*

Thank God, Robert was wearing a long frock coat with flapping tails. Brahms grabbed one, but it started to tear. Then he grabbed the other, which thankfully took the strain as Brahms hauled him down – and held him down, with Robert struggling violently to get up again.

Despite appearances Brahms was strong, very strong; all those years of arm-wrestling with young merchant seamen finally paid off. Soon Schumann was a spent force, silently gazing over Brahms's shoulder at something high in the sky, out of sight. The young Brahms looked around. Incredibly, the place was deserted, thank God. Schumann became as still as a corpse.

Brahms got to his feet. Now he was the trembling one. *What to do?* His mind was a blank. Then he remembered – some gossip he'd overheard at Liszt's camp court in Weimar. Whisperings about Robert's mental state – rumours he'd put down to pure bitchiness, for it was a well-known fact that so far as Liszt's arse-licking fans were concerned, next to the Master it was Wagner who was 'flavour of the month', while Schumann was very much not their cup of tea at all. 'Pure camomile, darling.' And hadn't Schumann's beloved sister taken a walk by stepping out of a third-floor window? Maybe it ran in the family.

Christ, I hope not, Brahms said to himself as he gently helped the sick man to his feet. The very thought of the 'S' word was enough to send shivers down his spine . . . ever since a certain awful night in the slums of Hamburg.

Down to practicalities and what to do now, for Christ's sake. 'Let's go home, Robert,' he said for lack of inspiration. 'It's nearly time for tea.'

Much to his relief the sick man allowed himself to be led like a child off the bridge, along the riverside footpath, across the park and into the house without incident. Whereupon Brahms, who was a confirmed atheist, breathed a sigh of relief and offered up a silent prayer.

FIVE

Seance

T HEY WERE ALL in bed, Marie, Elise, Julie, Ludy, Ferdy and Eugenie. No, not the same bed, though there was sharing: teenagers Marie and Elise shared, as did nine-year-old Julie and three-year-old Eugenie; as did five-year-old Ferdinand and six-year-old Ludwig. Cook in the attic was in bed, as was Robert in the master bedroom – heavily sedated.

Brahms and Clara sipped chocolate in the kitchen. 'He has his good days and he has his bad days,' Clara said, 'and I'm afraid the bad days are becoming ever more frequent. Almost anything can trigger them off – a beautiful flower, a crippled veteran. He sees the entire world in terms of music. Music of tranquillity, music of conflict. There was a time when his head was full of heavenly choirs; now it seems that a chorus of demons is in command and serenity is banished by cacophony. It becomes increasingly unbearable, driving him to acts of uncontrollable violence.'

Clara noticed Brahms's growing alarm. 'Don't worry. He hasn't hurt me or the children. He takes it out mainly on his manuscripts. Tears them to shreds. I'm at my wits' end. Help me!'

Helping people was not Brahms's forte. Coming from a humble background – his dad was a jobbing cornet player – he had only kept body and soul together by looking after number one. 'Has he seen a doctor?' he asked lamely.

'He's seen dozens,' said Clara with only slight exaggeration.

'What do they recommend?' asked Brahms.

'Everything from cold baths to nettle soup and brandy,' she replied with a wan little smile.

Robert stood in the doorway. He, too, was smiling. 'Time for a seance. Time to hook up with the three Bs,' he said, looking at Brahms, who noticed that Clara had turned pale.

Brahms made a wild guess. 'Bach, Beethoven and Buxtehude?'

'Close.' Robert smiled. 'Bach, Beethoven and Brahms. Buxtehude's old hat.'

'But why me?' said Brahms. 'I'm not an old master.'

'Just a matter of time, old son,' replied Schumann. 'Just a matter of time. Clara, bring the candles.'

As he turned and walked away, Clara went to a kitchen drawer and rummaged around for candles.

'If this is going to be an attempt to contact the dear departed I must ask to be excused,' said Brahms. 'Phantoms tend to freak me out.'

'You've attended seances before?' asked Clara.

'After the death of a lady friend,' muttered Brahms.

'And did you succeed in raising her spirit?' asked Clara tentatively.

Brahms nodded. 'And it was not a pretty sight, believe me.'

'Well, so far we've only succeeded in raising voices that Robert alone can hear. I'm hopeless. All I ever hear is the children upstairs. But you are definitely in touch with something that's out of reach to most of us. You're on a different plane, or so Robert thinks, so I'm afraid you have no option. Come along now.'

It was an order Brahms couldn't refuse. The fact that he got to hold Clara's hand as the participants formed the 'circle of light' was a bonus that communicated a current of desire deep down among the folds of his well-worn underpants. He was blushing again, a fact the flickering candles did not reveal, thank God, because Clara was looking straight at him – or was it straight through him? Robert was also staring straight through him. It was the most odd sensation. What was happening?

He felt possessed, taken over, as if his soul was not his own. The room was spinning and spinning – or was it he? Then he was falling, falling, falling, and there was music, magnificent music – none other than Beethoven's Tenth Symphony, in fact. Except that Beethoven had unfortunately never lived to write more than nine.

SIX

Fan City

*C*LARA FAIRLY ROMPED through the Davidsbundler Dances down at the old town hall. Brahms sat between teenagers Marie and Elise, the only Schumann children who could be relied upon not to jump up and down on their seats and make a scene. As aspiring soloists themselves, they were sufficiently advanced to appreciate the nuances of Mama's inimitable interpretation of Papa's marvellous music.

Brahms gave them a gentle nudge and indicated with a subtle rolling of the eyes a personage further along the row turning quite green with envy. Yes, it was Franz Liszt, star of every trendy salon, stage and stately home from St Petersburg to Paris. The girls grinned and then applauded wildly along with Brahms as Clara brought the piece to a triumphant close.

The applause was overwhelming. Clara brushed it aside as if it were her due and held a finger to her lips for silence.

'Thank you. I only hope I did my husband's music justice,' she said and glanced at the back of the hall where Robert was standing. All heads turned and all hands applauded once more as the grateful composer gave his gracious wife the 'thumbs up' sign.

Clara blew him a kiss and said, 'But there is more than one genius here tonight.' At this Franz Liszt preened himself and prepared to take a bow. 'His name is Johannes Brahms, and once I have familiarized myself with his idiom I will introduce a selection of his brilliant studies in my next recital here. Joe, take a bow.'

Brahms blushed (again) and reluctantly got to his feet – to scattered applause, save for the teenage fans either side of him, who more than made up for it. Liszt, too, was generous with his clapping, which surprised Brahms somewhat as he knew Liszt had never really forgiven him for sleeping through a rendition of his new Sonata in One Movement.

No, he's just trying to draw attention to himself, thought Brahms.

'And the one and only Franz Liszt has also honoured us with his presence tonight.'

No need to ask him to take a bow. He was on his feet in a shot, flamboyantly acknowledging the rapturous ovation that followed. It was overpowering. Several young ladies swooned just at the sight of him, including Marie and Elise. Now it was the turn of Brahms to turn green with envy.

'Franz, could I invite you to join me in bringing the evening's recital to a close? I'm sure your fans would be delighted, and as a fan myself, well, it would be a tremendous honour and a treasured memory.'

Without a moment's hesitation Liszt gave a slight bow and bounded up the aisle towards the stage. Bastard, thought Brahms to himself. He should have refused – graciously, of course. It's Clara's night, and here he is about to steal her thunder.

Liszt kissed Clara's hand and sat down on the spacious piano bench, effectively masking her from the audience.

'What shall it be, Franz?' asked Clara genially.

'You choose,' said Liszt gallantly.

'No, you choose,' insisted Clara.

'Let's leave it to the audience then,' proposed Liszt as he turned towards them. 'What'll it be?'

Cacophony followed as everyone yelled out their favourite opus number. 'Chopsticks!' shouted Marie and Elise, who had miraculously recovered from their swoon. Brahms meanwhile sank lower and lower in his seat, wishing himself elsewhere.

'It seems the First Hungarian Rhapsody has the biggest vote. What do you say, Clara?'

'Fine by me, Franz. Let's take it away.'

With a nod from the composer, who was undoubtedly the Liberace of his day, Clara started pounding the bass notes that signalled the ponderous introduction. But as the piece progressed she was reduced to providing the accompaniment, as Liszt pumped up the tempo and conjured from the keyboard fistfuls of Magyar magic and pounding peasant rhythms all dressed up in scintillating scales and glittering glissandi – real foot-tapping stuff, which evolved irresistibly into infectious hand-clapping as the rhythms grew ever racier. Brahms had never heard anything like it. It was like a bloody circus! Why not bring in the performing seals and red-nosed clowns? If it wasn't for Clara, who might have misinterpreted his actions, he would have got up and stamped out of the hall as ostentatiously as possible.

As it was he suffered in silence as the triumphant couple took bow after bow, until the audience finally let them go. The girls ran off to congratulate Mama and beg Uncle Franz to autograph their programmes. Only then did Brahms get to his feet and, avoiding all contact with the family, stride out into the dimly lit streets, fuming and looking for something to fuck.

SEVEN

Cook's Afternoon Off

*C*OOK'S AFTERNOON OFF was Brahms's busiest day. His morning was spent down at the music academy, coaching Marie and Elise on a broken-down piano in a practice room Clara had cadged gratis from the principal. She would be at home, practising on the exquisite hand-painted baby grand Robert had presented to her as an engagement present; or pounding away on a dummy keyboard in the bedroom, if the muse had inspired Robert to attempt composition.

Then it was back to the house for a light lunch for all the family around the kitchen table, after which Joe was on his own – with six children to amuse, out of the house. And it was winter. But fortunately it was a bright, sunny day, so a trip to the zoo might be in order.

'Oh, no, Uncle Joe,' wailed Marie when he suggested the idea. 'Do let's go to the circus instead. It's only here for a couple of days, and we've all got pocket money saved up specially.'

So it was decided. And Brahms was only too happy to comply. For though the monkey house at the zoo was nice and warm some of the orang-utans' antics needed a lot of explaining and invariably brought on his blushes again. Pictures of Robert and Clara popped into his mind, unbidden, getting up to the same sort of tricks, free for once to indulge their sexual fantasies without fear of discovery. How he longed to be a fly on the bedroom wall on such occasions, with great big goggle eyes but a small enough visage for his blushes to pass unnoticed.

At the circus there were red-nosed clowns, bare-backed riders and performing seals and an enthusiastic band playing a Hungarian rhapsody by Liszt. (That guy got everywhere.)

Inevitably, Brahms's thoughts returned to the night of the concert and his growing infatuation with the mother of the brood now surrounding him, captivated by the show. As he studied the children one by one, his mind ran riot in conjuring up pictures connected with their conception. Marie was the first born, on the verge of puberty and cute as a button. Very straightforward, that genesis: after an overlong courtship there was a veritable explosion of pent-up passion on the floor of the honeymoon suite, with the groom still in his top hat and the bride lying there with her legs wide open and her dress pulled up over her head.

Then eighteen months later came the perky Elise: this time the copulating couple were in bed naked but still in the tried and trusted missionary position.

Two years passed before it was the turn of shy little Julie. By this time Brahms's imagination had clothed husband and wife in nighties, with Clara's thrown (mask-like) over her head as Robert with his garment pulled up to the required height pumped away like a steam engine.

Then came sickly Emil, who never lived to blow out the candles on his second birthday cake, so he didn't count.

Then Brahms's glance went to the eldest boy, Ludwig, conceived two years later. A bit of a handful was Ludy, bit of a fidget, always trying to dominate. For this coupling Brahms imagined Clara on top, riding Robert like a Red Indian on a pinto pony. 'Ludwig, stop pulling Ferdy's hair!' shouted Brahms above the sound of the circus band.

Ferdinand was a sweetheart, devoted to his Labrador puppy, which led Brahms logically to the image of Mummy and Daddy going at it doggy fashion. Woof, woof.

Eighteen months separated the birth of the boys, before Eugenie, the last, arrived on the scene two and a half years later. Brahms's speculation on the manner of her conception was cut short by the dampening of his left trouser leg. No, it was not an unwelcome orgasm induced by wishful thinking; it was simply due to the saturated nappy of the last-mentioned mite balanced precariously on his knee. He wondered if the circus provided nappy-changing facilities but rather doubted it. Not that he carried spare nappies around with him, but he might consider sacrificing his cravat; or, better still, Marie's scarf, which had far more body to it.

Then Eugenie started to cry, which fortunately coincided with the grand finale – choreographed to yet another Hungarian rhapsody by Liszt. Such crass vulgarity! He'd show them. Some day he'd write a complete set himself, capturing the true Magyar spirit without descending to the bombast of the circus.

'Button up your coats, children,' he said briskly. 'Time to go.'

EIGHT

Time Out

THE SIGHT OF the ormolu clock in the middle of the lawn brought a chorus of conjecture from the children as they poured through the garden gate on their return home.

Brahms worked it out right away as he took in the broken window through which it had obviously been pitched. He smelled trouble, and his immediate concern was to shelter the children from it. Consequently he steered them into the back garden, where an ancient summer-house had been converted into a spacious and well-equipped playroom.

As he lit the oil lamp to banish the approach of evening shadows, he fielded the barrage of awkward questions and left Marie in charge, while he hurried off to investigate.

The house was devoid of light and life as he made his way into the twilit kitchen. He found a candle and lit it, stuck it in a holder and made his way cautiously along the passage towards the room with the broken window.

'Hello,' he called out in a voice as unsteady as the flickering flame. 'Is anyone at home?'

No answer. He tiptoed to the open door and listened intently. There was a sound, a very faint sound, as of an unidentifiable creature desperately scratching at something with fearfully sharp claws. It was disturbing.

Brahms hesitated and, for a moment, considered extinguishing the candle and creeping back the way he had come. Then something alien kicked in, akin to the something that had made him break into song at the front gate on the day of his arrival. Whatever it was, it propelled him through the wimp barrier and into the room, ready to confront the unknown, be it man or mouse.

The candle revealed an unexpected sight that caused a sharp intake of breath. Watery moonlight shone on the dim figure of a naked man seated at the piano. It was Robert attacking a piece of manuscript with a scratchy old pen.

'Put that light out,' he said abruptly. 'This is not for the sight of mortal eyes.'

Brahms obeyed and advanced tentatively towards the hieroglyphics, blots and scribbles with which the demented composer was feverishly covering the manuscript. There were eyes, suns, stars and sexual organs, swords, lips, snakes and ladders and a host of weird shapes and signs, the meaning of which Brahms could only guess at, all laid out like the music score of some insane symphony eating away at the mind of his unfortunate friend.

'Of course, I shall have to teach the players the new nomenclature,' Robert said, confidentially. 'New music needs a new syntax. How else can we even hope to express the inexplicable? Could you get me a cup of coffee, Joe? Cook's running a little late.'

Gratified at being presented with a safe means of escape from such a shattering encounter, Brahms said, 'Of course. I forget, do you take sugar?'

'Two lumps, if you please,' Robert replied with a smile. 'Though heaven knows I shouldn't. I'm trying to give it up.' And he continued his composition as Brahms thankfully left the room.

In the passageway Brahms collapsed against the wall, his mind racing. Should he get a doctor? Should he see if Clara was safe? And what about the children? They'd be indoors clamouring for their supper any moment. He was tempted to call out Clara's name but, fearful as to how Robert would react, decided to investigate in silence. He crept upstairs and started looking in the eerily quiet rooms.

All were in darkness, save for the master bedroom, from which a warm glow emanated. Brahms extinguished the candle and softly trod towards the open door. What would he see? A decapitated Clara, drowned in a sea of blood? Or maybe she'd be blindfolded and tied up. Hellish images from the rough waterfront of his youth all but flooded his thoughts.

What he actually saw, he was quite unprepared for – something in the shape of a ball, hidden beneath the bedclothes. Gingerly he pulled them back, and there was Clara, curled up in her nightie in the foetal position with her eyes tight shut. Her fists gripped a little bedroom clock.

Before she could open her eyes there was a sound at the door. Brahms spun around. It was Robert, clutching his manuscript.

'I've changed my mind,' he said evenly. 'I'll forgo the sugar. Give me a shot of brandy instead.'

For a moment Brahms froze; then, as Robert failed to remark on the situation, he nodded, covered Clara up again and quickly left the room as Robert walked in.

Before Brahms had reached the foot of the stairs he heard a noise from the kitchen. It sounded like Cook and the children.

NINE

Deception

*B*RAHMS NEVER NEEDED an alarm clock in the Schumann household. Daily from the crack of dawn scales drifted up the stairwell and sounded as clearly as a knock on his attic door.

The two eldest boys were supervised by the two eldest girls for an hour before breakfast every day except Sunday – ad infinitum; there was was a timetable pinned up on the kitchen wall that everyone knew by heart. Regular lessons were given in the summer-house, which also acted as a schoolroom under the supervision of a private tutor called Mr Somerfeld, a corpulent little fellow the children loved.

And Mother and Father took it in turns to do their own music-making. But today was an exception. Clara said she was going shopping and needed Brahms to come along to help her with the packages. This suited Robert very well, as he had a new musical dictionary to review for his private newspaper. Marie was to stand in as secretary, with strict instructions that the patient was to leave the house only over her dead body. But Robert seemed to be his old self again and determined to knuckle down to a day of dictation. When Brahms and Clara left soon after breakfast he was as happy as Larry.

The shopping spree was, of course, an excuse. Instead they made for a quiet coffee-house, where the distraught Clara quickly put Brahms in the picture regarding the events of the previous day. Naturally there was no mention of fun and games in the bedroom, though Clara did mention that they were both upstairs when Robert became upset by the ticking of a clock, the sound of which was interfering with the germ of a melody that was running unbidden through his brain. Thinking he was simply referring to the bedroom clock she tried to stop it and, failing to do so, buried it under a pillow in the bed.

Still Robert insisted that he could hear the tick and told her to do better.

Seeing that he was becoming more agitated by the moment, she half-jokingly suggested adopting the pose Brahms found her in some time later. This seemed to pacify Robert for a moment, until it seemed an even louder ticking occurred, which he identified as the big ormolu clock downstairs in the music room. By now she was alarmed, especially as Robert ordered her to hold her clock even tighter, lest the smallest sound break through.

'Tick, tick, tick! Tighter, tighter, tighter!' he yelled, his voice becoming louder and more manic with every cry. 'Tighter, tighter, tighter!' he screamed, accompanying each word with a thump of his fist on her head and body, the bedclothes only partially cushioning the force of the blows.

Then with a frightening threat as to what would happen to her if she so much as moved a muscle, he ran downstairs to take care of the ticking of the ormolu clock, which had apparently become quite intolerable. Moments later she heard the crash that signalled the departure of the source of his paranoia – whereupon she had expected his imminent return and God knows what to follow.

By the time Brahms found her she was almost a nervous wreck. But since his appearance at the bedroom door Robert had been his old self.

What to do? Clearly the cold baths and nettle soup and brandy had not worked, so there seemed little point in calling in the doctors.

'Maybe he needs to get away,' suggested Brahms, 'take a holiday, go hiking, get out of the house; get some fresh mountain air in his lungs, get light-headed at five thousand metres.'

'And who's going to supervise him? I can't, I've got a full calendar of recitals ahead of me. Someone's got to pay the rent. No reflection on you, Joe.'

Despite the reassurance, Brahms felt a pang of guilt. The ball was in his court and he knew it. Reluctantly he played the game. 'Walked right into that one,' he said with a smile. 'Still, it's no hardship. I'm the original happy wanderer, and it would certainly give you a welcome break.'

'Forget about me. I can cope. It's the children I'm worried about, and, of course, Robert, poor soul.'

'There's only one thing that worries me,' cautioned Brahms. 'If he takes it into his head to jump again, he'd have plenty of opportunities on holiday and I might not be able to stop him.'

'You're absolutely right, and no way will I put you in danger. Forget it.'

Brahms thought about protesting but reconsidered – he had a vivid imagination, and the thought of two struggling men falling off the Jungfrau was indeed a sobering thought. 'I suppose we could get a straitjacket,' he suggested, as a poor substitute.

'Can you imagine the traumatic effect that would have on the children?' said Clara dismissively. 'No, he must go into a nursing home for treatment.'

Brahms shuddered. In his mind he translated this suggestion as, 'No, he must be committed to a madhouse and physical abuse.' It would probably be located in the mountains in a derelict castle full of screaming, dangerous lunatics, where the only treatment he could expect would be a savage beating and a withdrawal of bathroom privileges. Attitudes towards the mentally ill were still medieval, and patients were subjected to cruel mockery rather than therapeutic medical care.

Naturally he did not mention this to Clara.

Instead he ordered two more Irish coffees to stimulate thoughts for a satisfactory conclusion. Together he and Clara awaited the coffees' arrival in a painful silence, which was finally broken by the unexpected arrival of Marie – in tears.

'Daddy's disappeared,' she sobbed.

TEN

Carnival

*T*HE MOMENT THEY stepped into the street they were swept up in a nightmare. Grotesque figures with beaks, claws and flashing fangs, acting like beasts of prey, swooped down and seized them and dragged them, vehemently protesting, into a wild bacchanalian revelry. For an instant Brahms imagined he'd been sucked into his mad friend's fervid mind.

In reality it was the one day in the year the generally staid city let its hair down and went crazy. The 26th of February was a date to remember. Clara invariably stayed at home whenever that day came around, preferring to indulge in Robert's lofty version of Carnavale at the keyboard, rather than descend to the depths of the gutter, where the majority of legless revellers found their true level.

This time, all shook up, Clara and Brahms fought their way home. They progressed into the music room, where they found Robert lying on the *chaise-longue* wrapped in a blanket, shivering like the plague and staring fixedly at the ormolu clock on the chimney-piece. His regular doctor was calmly taking his pulse.

Later, in the kitchen, the doctor took Clara and Brahms into his confidence while Marie and Cook kept watch over the stricken man. 'I've taken the liberty of sending my man to Endenich,' said the doctor solemnly, 'to ascertain if they can take Mr Schumann.'

'What's at Endenich?' queried Brahms.

'A safe haven where he will receive care and attention,' said the doctor. A nut house, he thought to himself.

'If that means I have to commit my own husband, you can forget it,' said Clara firmly.

'If it's any consolation, madame, it's his own most fervent desire,' said the doctor.

'What actually happened?' asked Brahms, more in an effort to give Clara time to come to terms with this latest bombshell than from a desire to learn the sad facts.

'He jumped off the Ritter bridge just over an hour ago and was dragged out of the water by some fishermen as the current swept him against the hull of their boat. It was a miracle,' said the doctor.

More like bloody good luck, thought Brahms.

'And as it was carnival time there were plenty of witnesses, so fortunately he was quickly identified when they carried him ashore. Thanks to the generosity of a philanthropic citizen who bequeathed his carriage, Mr Schumann was home in no time. And thanks to the perspicacity of your cook, madame, I was able to administer a sedative shortly after.'

Clara nodded her gratitude and said, 'We must get him into some nice warm clothes. It's cold out today.'

And so was settled the fate of Brahms's new friend – a friend he had barely got to know. As he stood by him in the garden a few hours later he wondered what words of comfort he could offer, as Robert gathered a small bouquet of hardy winter pansies. This was a situation quite new to him and one he had never anticipated. He had no frame of reference and could only think of a string of platitudes such as 'I'll come and visit. You'll be home in no time. Don't worry about the kids, I'll take good care of them. And don't worry about Clara, I'll really take good care of her.' Wisely, he kept these thoughts to himself, the last of which caused him some concern. Could he trust himself not to make a pass at her, knowing that her man was locked up and knowing that as a highly sexed and healthy woman she might soon begin to miss her nooky and become seducible?

Robert smiled up at him, almost as if he could read Brahms's thoughts and would generously bestow his blessing.

And Brahms smiled right back in gratitude.

'I'd like you to give these to Clara on my behalf,' said Robert, handing him the bouquet. 'I don't think I could bear to say goodbye to her in person. It just seems too final. And I do intend to come back, I assure you. And should any other man as much as look at her, please tell him I will not rest until I have nailed his testicles to the tallest tree in the Black Forest.'

Brahms almost burst a blood vessel trying not to blush.

ELEVEN

Seminar

'WHERE'S DADDY?' burbled baby Eugenie at the supper table that night. Brahms took a sip of the bortsch that Cook had just plonked before him and looked at the troubled little faces staring at him for an answer. In the absence of Clara, who was lying down, he was suddenly head of the family. This realization gave him no pleasure whatsoever. He loathed responsibility.

Marie gave him a challenging look; she alone of the children knew the facts. Out of sight beneath the table her leg was pressing against his own, warning him to fuck up at his peril. Well, that's how he interpreted it at the time ... but maybe he was wrong.

'Where Daddy!' persisted baby Eugenie, banging the high chair with her soup spoon.

'Daddy's gone on holiday,' said Brahms, desperately fighting for time.

'Without Mummy?' came the murmurs of disbelief.

Brahms's mind went blank. Marie came to the rescue.

'Mummy's very busy at the moment,' she said. 'She has lessons to give every day and a very important recital next week. So there. Daddy's just tired.'

'Tired,' said Ludy. 'How can he get tired just staring out of the window, for Chrissakes?' And while Brahms speculated on the source of Ludy's vocabulary, it was Elise who answered this time.

'He's looking up at the sky, shithead. Where else do you think all that heavenly music comes from?'

'From my arse,' Ferdy replied, giving her the finger – which shocked Brahms still further, as the two boys rocked with laughter.

'Watch your mouth, you dirty little sod,' screamed Marie, letting her hand fall on Brahms's knee.

Poor man. The unshockable boy from the brothels of Hamburg was deeply shocked, and he continued to speculate on the origin of the lewd lingo. For a moment he was tongue-tied, and only by summoning up that indefinable 'something' was he finally able to break through the dumb barrier.

'Shut the fuck up, the lot of you,' shouted Brahms through the din, 'and listen to me.'

Now it was the kids' turn to be shocked into silence.

'I'll be the first to admit your dad writes heavenly music, and we all know Clara plays like an angel. But, wait a minute, what on earth am I saying? I've never been to heaven, and I've never seen a real angel play. So what am I talking about? And maybe heavenly music is for God's ears alone, but can we really be sure that God actually has ears? Maybe he listens through his nose, or his arsehole – if he has one.'

Here the children tittered.

'And as for the angels, they're not born with a harp in their hands, are they? Can you imagine the noise all those beginners must make, plucking away up there like a bunch of pizzicatoed porcupines. It must be sheer hell.'

There were a few gasps at this, too.

'Anyway, how do we know they really play harps?' he asked. 'Maybe they play birds or fish or animals. Or maybe they make music out of rainbows, wind and rain; or maybe they exist purely as music themselves – all different kinds of music, from folk to futuristic. Why not? With God all things are possible. I believe Robert has discovered what no man has ever heard before – the real music of the heavens, which is so different from anything we can possibly imagine that he has to find a different way to write it down. Now that's not easy. It will take him time. He'll need peace and quiet. It could even take years. But in the end he'll find a way, believe me, a way to bring heaven on earth.'

'Fuck me!' said Cook in spontaneous appreciation, crossing herself as Marie impulsively applauded and the others joined in.

'Goodnight, sleep tight,' said Brahms blithely, heading for the door.

'Make sure the fleas don't bite,' chorused the children after him.

TWELVE

Nocturnal Admissions

HALF PAST SEVEN, said the ormolu clock in the music room, which was still miraculously ticking away. For a moment Brahms considered tickling the ivories, but that might disturb Clara, who was resting in her boudoir.

He speculated on her state of mind. She must be devastated, poor thing. She'd been in close proximity to Robert since the age of thirteen – over twenty years. It must be like losing a limb. The amputation had been brutal, with no anaesthetic to dull the pain.

They had come for him late in the afternoon. Brahms had helped Cook to load a large portmanteau of Robert's things on to the back of the carriage that was to take him away, while Clara had watched from an upstairs window, clutching the little bouquet of winter pansies that had been his farewell gesture. A swift handshake from Brahms, a boost from the keepers to assist Robert aboard, and he was gone as the pansies grew wet with Clara's grief.

By now the hush of mourning had enveloped the house. Brahms let himself imagine his chances of being accepted by Clara as a temporary substitute to cling to. Temporary? The odds were that Robert had been issued a one-way ticket and they'd seen the last of him, for there were to be no visitors until further notice.

Brahms wondered what had brought his new friend to such a sorry impasse. He knew of similar cases from his education in the school of sleaze he had attended in Hamburg. There had been an isolated house down by the docks full of demented sailors with their dicks falling off through contact with the syphilitic sylphs who had been his friends.

Brahms wondered if Robert had ever enjoyed the fruits of promiscuity. Had frustration, induced by the proximity of the hot crumpet he may have been denied a taste of, driven him to seek a shop-soiled substitute elsewhere? It was a distinct possibility with which Brahms could completely sympathize. He shuddered. If that were the case, what about Clara? Had she also caught the clap? The thought was a big turn-off.

So far he'd been lucky. The brothel-keepers of his acquaintance had treated him kindly by procuring for him a steady stream of healthy virgins. Yes, he'd been thoroughly spoiled, but that was one of the perks of the job. Then he remembered the night of the concert and his overwhelming desire to spill his frustration into a *demoiselle de la nuit*. But he'd enjoyed her 'in armour', so touch wood . . . For a moment he stopped daydreaming and got practical.

What about Clara's spotless reputation? With her husband out of the way and a young man about the house, tongues were bound to wag, and that would do neither of them any good. Yet it was clear she needed moral support, for the moment at least, and the kids would certainly benefit from the influence of a sympathetic father figure. And where else would he find free lodgings and three square meals a day? So he made a decision – to play it by ear and hope for the best.

He sighed as he crept past Clara's room to the sound of sobbing. He hesitated. Should he knock and possibly open a can of worms or keep going? He kept going. Early to bed, early to rise. He cursed his erection and willed himself to sleep with the help of an imaginary metronome that slowly ticked but never tocked.

In no time he was asleep, dreaming of Marie at the table with her hand on his knee and beginning to climb higher. Then he woke up, half expecting to find her in bed with him – in which case he would have encountered the aroma of eau-de-Cologne. But a couple of deep breaths soon put an end to that little fantasy. The perfume he smelled was far more erotic, very French, very expensive and very Clara.

Her lips found his, her tongue was halfway down his throat. For a moment the spectre of syphilis raised its raddled head, to be dispelled immediately as her hand, cold as marble, closed around his penis. A moment later he had a leg over.

THIRTEEN

Cradle Song

*A*T LEAST THERE was no risk of her getting pregnant, because she was well and truly pregnant already. But after the birth of yet another mouth to feed they would have to be more careful.

There was more to their relationship than sex. They shared a deep affection for each other, based upon their mutual respect for their individual artistry. Clara's growing mastery of Brahms's idiom encouraged him to new heights of composition. And then there was the young man's interaction with the children, who tended to look upon him as an older brother rather than another parent.

As for Robert, there were monthly reports on his progress, for there *was* progress – and the possibility of visits, should it be maintained.

Brahms noticed that Marie was glaring at him. She was sitting on a chair near the door of the music room as he tickled the ivories of Clara's baby grand.

'You're a bad boy. She's old enough to be your mother,' said Marie out of the blue.

Brahms was shocked but not surprised. He'd guessed she was aware of his and Clara's liaison, but this was the first time she had brought it into the open.

'Bad boys deserve spanking,' he replied, smiling.

'Then drop your trousers,' she said teasingly.

Brahms didn't miss a beat, as he went on softly playing his delectable 'Cradle Song' and considered his reply. Many possibilities flashed through his mind, 'I'll drop mine if you drop yours' being first and foremost.

As things transpired he was spared the embarrassment, the cry of a new-born baby coming to the rescue. Marie was out of the door and up the stairs in an instant. Brahms continued playing, speculated on the sex of the new arrival and shuddered at the possibility of twins.

'Mummy says you can all come up now,' shouted Marie down the stairwell.

Brahms played a final 'plonk, plonk' and joined the throng of youngsters racing up to greet offspring number eight.

'It's a boy,' said the doctor genially, as he passed Brahms on the landing, 'a healthy, blue-eyed, bouncing boy.'

'How's Madame Schumann?' asked Brahms.

'All things considered . . .' He paused. 'I'm afraid I'm not at liberty to say. Patient confidentiality, you understand. She needs rest. I'll call again tomorrow morning. Good day.'

'Hello, Felix,' cried the kids, clambering all over Clara's rumpled bed.

Poor woman, thought Brahms, and his heart hardened towards the cruel bastard who had forced the frail creature through eight painful deliveries and put her life at risk, regardless. Well, hopefully he'd done it for the last time. Thank God he was behind bars.

'All right, children,' he said aloud. 'Mummy's tired. So downstairs, every-one, or we'll all be late for the party.'

'What party?' they chorused.

'Felix's birthday party, of course. What else?'

They all cheered. Young Eugenie fell off the bed and started howling. Brahms scooped her up and started herding everyone towards the door. 'Say goodnight,' said Brahms, as Cook came in with a tray of light refreshments.

'Goodnight, Mummy. Goodnight, Baby Felix,' said the children, blowing kisses as they left the room. Brahms took their cue and did likewise, to which Clara responded with a wan smile. Then as Cook fixed a napkin and prepared to spoon-feed her, Joe patted Eugenie comfortingly on the head, started downstairs and wondered if a kitchen candle stuck in a stale slice of apple strudel would pass muster as a birthday cake.

Something caught his eye at the foot of the stairs. It looked like a hanky. He stooped to pick it up. Heavens above – it was a pair of knickers. Hastily he stuffed them into his trouser pocket and hurried on, blushing.

FOURTEEN

Farewell Performance

*I*T WAS A full house. Marie nursed baby Felix on the *chaise-longue* next to Joe. Eugenie sat on Cook's knee, while Elise sat cross-legged on the floor between Ludy and Ferdy. Julie hovered nervously in the doorway and, unlike her siblings, was dressed in her Sunday best.

It was a command performance. Clara was about to begin an extensive tour. As usual she had cast her magic spell, which effectively turned noisy brats into mute little angels and godless adults into worshippers at her shrine.

Cook beamed as Clara chased butterflies up and down the keyboard, and Brahms held his breath for fear of disturbing their play – until a thundering on the front door suddenly killed them dead.

'Shit,' said Joe, as chaos reigned.

'He's early,' said Clara, glancing at the clock. 'No, he isn't. Julie, ask him to wait. Cook, help him with the luggage, will you?'

Cook swung little Eugenie into Marie's arms and everyone spilled into the hall, all talking at once.

'Now, girls, remember what I told you,' said Clara.

'Yes, Mama,' replied the two eldest in unison. 'I'm to make sure the boys are in bed by seven,' continued Elise. 'And I'm to make sure they have their piano lessons every day,' added Marie.

'And I'm to make sure the young ladies are in bed by eleven and have their piano lessons every day,' joked Brahms.

'And to give them a good spanking if they disobey,' said the girls.

'And to give them a good spanking if they disobey,' said Brahms, giving them a wink.

'And don't forget the autographs, Mother,' said Ferdy, 'specially the Empress of Russia.'

'And Queen Victoria, Mummy. You simply must get hers,' Ludy insisted.

'I'm sure your mama, as undisputed queen of the keyboard, will be far too busy signing her own to worry about those old ducks,' said Brahms.

'I'll try to remember, my dears, I really will. I promise.'

Then it was goodbyes all round, especially for Julie, who was to be dropped off in Berlin as company for Granny.

'Take care,' said Brahms, giving Clara a peck on the cheek, 'and don't worry, I'll look after them.' Clara was uncharacteristically stumped for a reply, so kissed him full on the mouth, which said more than any words she might have uttered.

A minute later they were all at the garden gate waving goodbye and shouting *'Bon voyage.'* Then it was all back to the music room for a rowdy game of musical chairs to a selection of Joe's Hungarian rhapsodies.

'Break it up,' said Brahms after a while. 'You're getting too rough. We've just got time for a short game before lunch. What'll it be?'

'Kiss in the ring, kiss in the ring!' shouted Marie, giving Joe the eye.

FIFTEEN

Animal Farm

*C*ONTRARY TO HIS expectations, Endenich did not look like a medieval castle but more like a model farm, complete with barns and outbuildings, all visible through the bars of truly splendid gates. The entry would not have been out of place at a stately home, except for the anomaly of broken glass that crowned the high brick wall surrounding the property. Brahms peered through the wrought-iron filigree for signs of life, having failed to find any means of announcing his arrival.

Most odd. He had not expected, either, that his arrival would be heralded by the sound of music; but there it was, floating on the breeze. It put him in mind of dance nights spent in the Tyrolean Tavern in Hamburg. He considered shouting to attract attention, but in a direct contest with the band it would probably be a waste of breath.

Instead he did the last thing anyone would have thought of. He depressed the big iron handle – and the gate swung invitingly open. Closing it firmly behind him, he wondered if any of the inmates had ever done the same.

Following the strains of a lively polka, Brahms walked around a corner of the main building and found himself in a beautiful garden with a small band-stand on which . . . yes, it was. Yes, Robert was conducting a mixed group of musicians, and, strangely enough, they weren't too bad. Not as good as the regulars in the Tyrolean Tavern but, well, good enough to give the dozen or so dancing couples who encircled them a good strong beat.

'You must be Johannes Brahms,' said an unexpected voice behind him. 'My name is Dr Rosenberg.'

Brahms turned to see an elderly man who put him in mind of a mad doctor. Not that he had ever met one, but like most of us he had a ready-made image in mind, even down to the bald head, white coat and pebble glasses.

'Pleased to meet you,' said Brahms. 'Thanks for inviting me.'

'As his best friend, and in the absence of next of kin, I wanted you to see for yourself his progress towards rehabilitation.'

'It's extraordinary,' stammered Brahms. 'I would never have thought it possible.'

Brahms was even more surprised when Robert smiled at him and shouted, 'Why don't you come and join in?'

Brahms stood there nonplussed.

'I understand from Robert that you are familiar with the bugle,' said the doctor. 'Our man suffers from occasional short-term memory loss and has just suffered a relapse. As far as we know he is free of contagious disease, so you need have no fear of contamination in blowing his instrument. I'm sure your involvement would certainly add a little more texture to the overall orchestral tone.'

Bonkers, thought Brahms, but he nodded his acquiescence and, dodging through the dancing couples, approached the bandstand.

'Give us a kiss,' said Robert as Brahms brushed past him.

Brahms kissed him on the cheek and blushed, before taking his place among the inmates and picking up the abandoned instrument.

The cornet had been the first instrument the young Brahms had ever mastered, which is hardly surprising considering his dad had been a master bugler in the Hamburg Civic Guard and had made sure young Joe would be talented enough to take his place when it came time to retire. Well, things had taken a different path when the boy got turned on to the piano . . .

They were halfway through 'All the Nice Girls Love a Sailor' when Brahms pursed his lips to the brass mouthpiece and started to play. And if Miles Davis could have been a greenfly on the garden wall he would have turned greener with envy.

After a few bars the rest of the band stopped playing and gawked in admiration; so did the dancers. Robert, too, was entranced, and likewise the mad doctor, who considered offering him a job on the staff.

They just wouldn't let him go and began calling out their favourite tunes. Brahms obliged until he was breathless and, after a soulful rendition of 'The Last Roast of Summer', just had to call it a day.

All the same it had been an exhilarating experience, for, to tell the truth, he was beginning to feel as if he had been incarcerated in a madhouse himself – at times, at any rate. Naturally, we are referring to the Schumann residence.

Cook was a help, it's true, but her foul language was constantly making him homesick for the delights of his home town. And Marie was a terrible flirt, and it was a constant battle to keep his hands off her. Apart from that, she was a bad example for her younger sister Elise, who was developing daily.

As for the boys . . . well, Ferdy was all right, but Ludy – he'd been a forceps baby and could well have suffered brain damage to judge by his unpredictable behaviour. And Felix never seemed to stop crying. But thank God for little Eugenie, always as good as gold. He had a real soft spot for her. She was his favourite.

Lunch in the sanatorium's big hall started off well but eventually degenerated into custard pie throwing, which was not discouraged, though a damper was put on the fun when a hose trained on the perpetrators achieved two objectives – calming them down and cleaning them off.

Robert had a nice room overlooking the garden, furnished with a bed and a piano. There was also a small anteroom containing a commode and washing facilities. Incredible as it may seem, Brahms found himself actually beginning to envy his troubled friend, who now appeared to be far less troubled than him.

Seemingly his old self, he played Brahms a new composition that plunged into a radical direction, with unexpected key changes and ambiguous rhythms. It was positively revolutionary and opened a door in Brahms's mind that provided a glimpse into unexplored musical territory.

As he played, Schumann asked after the children, to which Brahms answered by painting an idyllic picture. A tear trickled down Robert's cheek at this, to be followed by yet another on the opposite side as he proudly produced an elegant scrapbook he'd compiled of Clara's grand tour, made up of reviews that Marie had cut out of various periodicals and posted off to him.

He's more sane than I am, thought Brahms to himself, as a knock on the door heralded the arrival of the mad doctor and two assistants.

'Time for your bath, Robert,' said the doctor.

'Well, Robert,' said Brahms, 'it's great to see you looking so good, and I look forward –'

'Oh, don't go yet,' said Robert urgently. 'We've nothing to hide, have we, doctor?'

The doctor hesitated before replying. 'I doubt Mr Brahms is familiar with this particular form of treatment and it might –'

'But he's from Hamburg,' interrupted Robert, laughing. 'And if he's not accustomed to it, it's about time he was.'

The germ of a memory stirred in Brahms's mind, causing an involuntary shudder. But before the germ could grow into a specific thought he found himself leaving the room arm in arm with Robert, and walking down a long corridor of closed doors.

At the end of the hallway they broke into single file and descended a flight of stairs to a windowless room in the basement. There a bleating lamb was shitting itself and a burly-looking man in a rubber apron was sharpening a butcher's knife. Brahms was about to experience yet another living nightmare.

'Stand well back, Joe,' warned Robert. 'Animal baths can be a bit messy.'

Suddenly the germ in Brahms's mind blossomed in a shower of blood as the butcher slit the lamb in two. A suddenly naked Robert immersed his private parts into its throbbing intestines, while the two keepers held its heaving carcass firmly position.

'Oh, the relief,' sighed Robert, close to ecstasy. 'The relief . . . Aah!'

SIXTEEN

Dear Joe

BRAHMS HAD GIVEN up all thoughts of composition in favour of baby-sitting. But he did manage to start cataloguing Robert's scores and collating numerous manuscripts stacked haphazardly all over the house. And his supervision of the music lessons of his charges turned what could have been a chore for all concerned into a treat to look forward to. But everyone knew it couldn't last for ever.

'What does she say?' asked Marie, as Brahms walked into the music room reading a letter.

'When is she coming home?' put in Elise.

Brahms glanced at the girls seated at the piano playing one of their father's many duets. 'She plans to return directly she's finished her grand tour of Great Britain, which becomes further extended daily as word of her consummate artistry spreads widely throughout the land. She's even taken tea with Queen Victoria at Windsor Castle.'

'I wonder if she remembered to get Ludy's autograph,' said Marie. 'He asks me every day.'

'She never got one from the Empress of Russia for poor Ferdy,' said Elise, 'so why should she bother with Ludy?'

'And she's been offered a tour of Scandinavia in July and August,' continued Brahms. Both girls stopped playing and glowered.

'That means Julie's going to be stuck in Berlin all summer and won't be able to join us at the seaside,' wailed Elise.

'And who do you think's going to take us to the seaside if she's swanning around Sweden?' demanded Marie, fixing her gaze on Brahms.

'Don't look at me,' he replied. 'I'm committed elsewhere.'

'What do you mean?' asked Elise apprehensively.

'You're not thinking of leaving,' said Marie menacingly.

'I've been offered a tour myself. Not on the grand scale of your mother's. Purely local.'

'Will you be coming here?' asked Elise.

'We could come and cheer you along,' said Marie hopefully.

Brahms shook his head. 'Fortunately not. I'd be compared to Clara, and not to my advantage. No, I'm in Hamburg, Kiel, Bremen and Leipzig, but at least it will give the public a chance to hear my music.'

'But Mummy's played your music in England, hasn't she?' asked Elise.

'And I won't be going there either,' said Brahms.

'You can't just abandon us,' said Marie with a hint of outrage, 'can you?'

'How can you even think such a thing?' said Brahms. 'But your mother has a proposal.'

'Hang on to your hats,' said Elise.

'If she wants to send us off to grumpy old Gramps, we're not going,' said Marie.

'We're putting our foot down,' said Elise with a little stamp.

'Relax, there's no fear of that,' said Brahms. 'She wants you to start singing for your supper.'

'Where! On street corners?' queried Elise.

'Or in a tavern?' said Marie. 'I wouldn't mind singing in a tavern.'

'There is a tavern in the town,' sang Brahms. 'Sorry, I was speaking metaphorically. Your mother suggests we get another piano – a cheap upright would do – and advertise for pupils so that you can start paying for your keep at last.'

'Killjoy,' said Elise.

'Skinflint,' added Marie. 'We're still only pupils ourselves.'

'We're not even qualified,' Elise pointed out.

'Nonsense. That rendition of your father's duet was faultless,' said Brahms.

'Only thanks to your coaching,' said Marie.

'And when the pupils play better than the teacher, it's time to quit.'

Somewhat mollified, the girls fell silent until Marie saw another snag. 'What about the boys? Are we expected to take care of them as well?'

'No. She wants them sent away to boarding-school.'

'Not Baby Felix, surely,' said Marie.

'No, Cook's in charge of Felix and little Eugenie, with a helping hand from you two. With me gone, Clara thinks you'll all have time on your hands.'

'What else did she say?' fumed Marie.

'Any other orders?' demanded Elise.

'No, but she did ask how often I've had to spank you,' said Brahms in an attempt to lighten the mood.

'Don't you wish,' said Elise.

'Dream on,' said Marie.

Brahms smiled. He was pleased with himself. He'd been a good boy, but then he had Hamburg to look forward to.

SEVENTEEN

Return of the Prodigal

BRAHMS WAS BORN in the heart of Hamburg's red-light district, and to that district he returned after his escape from Stalag Schumann in Stuttgart.

Nothing much had changed. His parents still occupied the modest house where he had been brought up with an elder sister Elisabeth and a younger brother Fritz. And though the boys had doubled up in bed as children they had well outgrown that possibility, and there was no spare room.

Doubtless he could have found a *pied-à-terre* in a high-class whorehouse, but that would have entailed performing, and he didn't want to be tied down, though he was sorely tempted by the hot and cold running crumpet always on offer. But surely it was time to put the indiscretions of youth behind him if he were to win the respect of the concert-going public.

So he went to stay with his old teacher Eduard Marksen who had recognized his pianist gifts even as a child, had supervised his spectacular progress ever since and had never asked for so much as a penny piece for this unstinting devotion. Moving into Marksen's put Brahms in the posh part of town in his own spacious room, with a lifestyle to which he would have liked to become accustomed.

An added bonus was that old Marksen himself was on hand to coach him for his début concert. The main work was to be Mozart's Concerto in D minor (K466), into which Brahms planned to introduce a cadenza that needed to be a showcase for his own unique style while remaining true to the spirit of Mozart.

Brahms sweated blood before the old man was satisfied. A Bach partita transposed for the left hand and his own Scherzo in E flat minor gave him far less trouble, but he had to work really hard to attack Robert's Carnavale with any confidence.

Brahms went for a long walk before arriving at the concert hall just minutes before curtain up. Ideally he would have preferred to walk through the
stage door and straight up to the keyboard. Indeed, he had once done just that
– in time to hear the manager announcing the cancellation of the concert
because of the 'indisposition' of the soloist.

Instead, he made it a practice now to utilize any spare time backstage
drumming his hands on his knees in a near-frenzied tattoo.

Most of the audience in the sparsely filled hall were there out of curiosity,
including old drinking companions and ladies of the town who had often
danced to his tune. There were also a handful of music lovers who had been
present at his début as an infant phenomenon, when he had wowed them with
an unforgettable rendition of Thalberg's Fantasia on Themes from Bellini's
Norma. Mind blowing! And naturally the family were present to give their
support, as were many of Dad's mates from the Civic Guard.

Then there were the thousand-odd members of the Hamburg Philharmonic Society, who were conspicuous by their absence because they could
never forgive Brahms his sordid antecedents. He'd show them! A day would
come when they'd kill for a ticket; one day he'd have them eating out of his
hand, licking his arse. Tonight was going to be the first step on the ladder
leading to fame, and nothing would stop him until he had climbed right to the
top to take his bow.

To scattered applause, which he acknowledged with a nod, he sat down to
play his Scherzo in E flat minor. As he struck the first chord his heart sank: the
piano was a semitone out of tune.

There were two options. He could either stop and ask if there was a piano
tuner in the house, or he could transpose the score as he played, which would
be just conceivable with a simple accompaniment to a song, but with a work of
the present complexity it was next to impossible.

He did not hesitate. Once committed he felt there was no course but to
continue. And, as things transpired, a computer could not have done better
(and most certainly would have lacked the artistry Brahms brought to his performance). The members of the audience in the front row, who wondered why
he was sweating so profusely on such a cool night, had little idea what a titanic
achievement they were privy to.

Only one other person in the hall had the remotest notion, and he, too, was
sweating. That was old Marksen. He knew right enough – and marvelled.

Four minutes later Brahms rose to his feet to a gratifying round of applause, for even if the audience knew nothing of a seemingly insurmountable hurdle brilliantly jumped they were acutely aware that they had witnessed something rather special. And they realized what he had done when Brahms explained the problem and put his question regarding the piano tuner, whereupon he received a standing ovation.

After the piano was set right, the remainder of the first half was a doddle, with the Mozart concerto almost playing itself. All the same, Brahms was happy to down a couple of pints during the interval, before returning to the stage eager to introduce his listeners to the fantastic world of Robert Schumann. Who should he see sitting in the front row but an attractive woman smiling up at him and applauding with the rest of the audience.

Shit! It was Clara!

EIGHTEEN

Magic Fire

BRAHMS DID A double-take. It couldn't be Clara. She was at Windsor Castle having a chin-wag with Her Royal Majesty. Maybe she'd had a horrible accident, been dead and buried and come back to haunt him. But did phantoms wink and adjust their dresses to show a shapely ankle?

Acting purely on impulse, Brahms winked back. Whoever she was – hallucination or flesh-and-blood human being – she looked like Clara, and he simply couldn't sit there and launch into a masterpiece she'd made her very own; he simply couldn't. It would be like rape. Consequently he rose to his feet for an improvised announcement.

'Ladies and gentlemen, as you will see from your programme, I had intended to finish with the Bach partita, but for reasons that will soon become evident I will start with it instead. Thank you.' And without further ado he sat down to play.

Thankfully, Brahms usually played in public without the need of a score, having familiarized himself with every note through constant practice and a striving for perfection. And that night it was just as well. For a full five minutes he was unable to tear his eyes away from that shapely ankle in the front row. As he flew through the piece on autopilot he wondered if this was a first – the first time Bach's sublime partita had ever been performed by an artist with a massive erection swinging like a fleshy metronome.

After the applause, taking a bow was a bit of a problem. He overcame it by rising to his feet all but bent double. Signalling for silence, he quickly sat down again and glanced at Clara, who was corpsing herself. Immediately, he averted his gaze and turned once again to the audience.

'Thank you. Tonight we are honoured with the presence of an artist who has made the next work very much her own; in fact, it was written expressly for her by her husband, Robert. Ladies and gentlemen, please give a warm welcome to an artist newly returned from England after a triumphant international tour, who has nevertheless found time to honour me with her presence here tonight. I give you ... Madame Clara Schumann.'

Mercifully, Brahms's erection had subsided, so he was able to stand upright as he drew attention to the object of the spontaneous applause.

Unlike most of her contemporaries, Clara was not a flamboyant extrovert, and there were some who thought her demeanour and mode of dress more fitting to the cloisters than the concert hall. So it was with some reticence that Clara rose to her feet and faced her admirers. And as she felt Brahms's gaze boring into her back she realized for the first time how intimidated he must feel at her sudden appearance. She hadn't planned it. It was a complete coincidence that they both happened to be in Hamburg at the same time. He'd written her with details of his upcoming tour but made no mention of dates, and it was only while booking into her hotel that she had happened to catch sight of a poster announcing the concert. After that she hadn't thought twice; it was a must. But it had been a mistake. Poor Joe, she could imagine his panic.

But could she really? Really feel the creeping paralysis beginning to exert its numbing grip? He felt like suggesting that she take over, he felt like running away, he felt just plain awful.

Then he felt something else. He felt a positive current of energy flowing towards him, generated by the goddess who had materialized in answer to an unuttered prayer. For to tell the truth he'd had growing reservations concerning Carnavale, doubts as to his ability to do it justice. He'd heard Robert play it and was also familiar with Clara's interpretation. In their different ways – and the differences were extremely subtle – they nevertheless complemented each other. Brahms loved them both and felt like an interloper, about to turn that precious harmony into discord. But Clara's telepathic intervention, be it spiritual or inspirational, was gradually dispelling his misgivings and filling him with ever-increasing confidence.

He resumed his seat and played like one possessed, because he was possessed. Passion surged through him, love surged through him, love for them both surged from his soul to his fingertips and found expression in the supersonic vibes that penetrated the very pores of every punter in the hall, the hard of hearing not excepted.

Later, in bed with Clara, there was shared immolation. Even Robert, miles away at Endenich, felt the warmth of its glow.

NINETEEN

Crisis

ONE YEAR LATER found the Schumann household busily preparing for the summer holidays. Everyone was at home. Julie was back from Berlin, the boys were back from school and Brahms had finally made order out of chaos with regard to Robert's manuscripts. Every last scrap of music had been painstakingly annotated and catalogued. And Clara, who was between engagements, had to concede that Marie and Elise had earned a bit of a break from the teaching treadmill.

As for the younger ones, well, they were in danger of going stir crazy. At last it seemed that the long-delayed trip to the seaside was about to be realized.

Then came a bolt from the blue. Robert was in a critical condition. This was kept from the children, but suddenly the holidays were on hold. Brahms and Clara left as soon as they could, amid much wailing and gnashing of teeth.

Little passed between them during the fifty-five-minute train journey to Endenich. Brahms's mind was in turmoil. Fragments of his friend's music came and went, as did feelings of guilt and remorse. He should have paid more frequent visits, especially since Robert seemed to derive increasing benefit from them.

He remembered the last one quite vividly. Dr Rosenberg had allowed them access to the grand piano in his private apartment, much to their mutual enjoyment. First Robert had cleared up a few points concerning interpretation of the Davidsbundler Dances, and the rest of the visit had been devoted to playing lively duets. Neither of them had wanted the occasion to end, and when the time had come for Brahms to leave he had prevailed on the good doctor to let Robert accompany him to the station. The doctor had come, too, in order to walk the patient back to the asylum.

'You will write a big choral work. I can hear it in my head. It will enjoy

enormous success.' These were the last words his friend had said to him, shouting to Brahms from the platform as the train chugged away into a glorious
sunset.

What's he doing in a madhouse? had been his thought, and not for the first
time, as he stared out the window of the moving train. He's perfectly sane.

Now he was returning on that same train to he knew not what.

Joe's personal diagnosis of Robert's condition made this urgent summons
all the more mystifying. That last visit had been little more than a month ago.
And the letters – they'd maintained a regular correspondence, discussing
everything from music to politics, without even the slightest hint of any mental
frailty on the part of his beloved friend. Why the sudden relapse? Perhaps it
was only momentary, and the sight of Clara could assuage it.

Oddly enough, she had never been permitted to see Robert, and though
she had asked to do so often enough Rosenberg had never given way or
offered a reason why. Perhaps he feared that a visit would disturb his patient's
tranquillity or even cause him to entertain thoughts of escape.

Brahms looked across at Clara. She was reading a newspaper she had
found in the carriage. What is she thinking about? Not the outcome of the
Crimean War, surely?

A shrill whistle announced their arrival.

TWENTY

Fairy-Tale

T HEY TOOK IT in turns to observe him through a peep-hole in the door. Clara went first, only to recoil in little over a second, her usual pallor turning to an even whiter shade of pale. Brahms lingered a little longer, finding it hard to comprehend the ravages suffered by his friend in four short weeks. True, Dr Rosenberg had given them fair warning, or thought he had, but nothing he might have said could have prepared them for the shocking reality. From a healthy-looking middle-aged man Robert had turned into a (barely) living cadaver.

Without ceremony Clara elbowed Brahms aside, opened wide the door, rushed into the room and threw herself upon the dying man. Brahms winced at the rasp of Robert's breath in response to this added pressure. His own shock kept him rooted to the spot. Robert might well die of suffocation, he thought, while I stand by and watch.

Dr Rosenberg acted quickly. With surprising strength he pulled Clara from Robert's bed and to her feet, holding her so tightly that she began to whimper – until suddenly she collapsed and would have fallen to the floor had the doctor not supported her and then gently guided her unsteady progress out of the room.

Slowly Brahms moved towards the bedside, under the eagle eye of a male nurse poised to thwart any further histrionics. Brahms simply took hold of his friend's skeletal hand. The attendant relaxed.

The physical contact seemed to calm and invigorate Robert at the same time, encouraging him to offer a word of explanation to the one man in the world he trusted. Brahms bent low to catch the sound. 'They are trying to poison me,' Robert whispered.

So that's it, thought Brahms. That's why he won't eat.

On Brahms's and Clara's arrival at the sanatorium the doctor had invited the visitors into his study to put them in the picture. 'Before I take you to see Mr Schumann, I must remark that your husband's inexplicable decline dates back to the last visit of our friend here,' he had said, giving Brahms a dirty look. 'That very evening, and for no obvious reason, the patient declined his supper. Nor would he partake of his breakfast the following day, nor his lunch, nor supper and so on and so on, with neither rhyme nor reason, up to the present day.'

'So, in plain words, he's on a hunger strike,' Clara had said.

The doctor had given a curt nod.

'Then why don't you resort to force-feeding?' Brahms had demanded.

'That is a barbaric practice frowned upon in this establishment,' the irate doctor had retorted. 'We like to look on ourselves as enlightened.'

Enlightened, my arse, Brahms had thought, calling to mind the 'animal bath' he'd witnessed.

'Why did you not inform us of this sooner?' Clara had said, her voice hardening.

'We were hopeful of a breakthrough,' the doctor had replied. 'We hoped to find the key that would unlock the door guarding his dark secret and expose it to the healing light of science.'

The man's delusional, Brahms had thought. Aloud, he had said, 'Have you ever considered that his behaviour might simply be a protest against institutional cuisine?'

'We've tried everything from pigs' trotters to caviare,' the doctor had replied with some heat. 'He simply spits it out.'

Then Clara had put in her ha'p'orth. 'I understand that he enjoyed a glimpse of freedom during my friend Mr Brahms's last visit. Is it possible, do you think, that this glimpse, brief as it was, could have driven him to despair?'

Thanks a lot, Brahms had thought. I'm the one that visited him, and I'm the one who'll be comforting the kids when he dies, too. For a moment he had almost hated the woman he loved.

Clara had tried to clarify her thoughts. 'Despair, doctor, at the thought that this brief encounter with the real world might well be his last. Isn't it possible that he should no longer wish to prolong the agony and meant to end it while the vision of beauty was still fresh in his mind?'

Neither Brahms nor the doctor had thought much of Clara's analysis, for different reasons.

'Our patients defy authority by whatever means available to them,' the doctor had asserted with finality. 'We can't read their minds –'

'Just let us see him,' Brahms had interrupted.

But as events transpired, Clara hadn't been that far off the mark, as Brahms was soon to discover.

'Who is trying to poison you?' asked Brahms in answer to Robert's frightening statement.

'You remember that evening I came to the station to see you off?' Robert asked, insistingly. 'Do you remember that blood-red sunset?'

Brahms nodded. So Clara was right; the scene had made an indelible impression on Robert. Perhaps she could read Robert's mind a little, the same way she could always interpret his music.

'You know the Seven Dwarves?' Again Brahms nodded. Like most locals he knew that the range of hills dominating the landscape at Endenich had been nicknamed the Seven Dwarves.

'Well, when I saw the Seven Dwarves rising above the trees on my return,' confided Robert, 'they were scarlet with blood.'

'Red sky at night, shepherd's delight,' said Brahms for lack of anything more inspired.

'And, of course, we all know who the Seven Dwarves keep in their thraldom, don't we?' said Robert conspiratorially.

'Snow White,' said Brahms, responding as if hypnotized to the very question he'd often put to this man's children during bedtime stories.

'Exactly,' sighed Robert, as though relieved.

What the devil . . . ? thought Brahms.

'And guess what,' Robert confided. 'A moment ago she came to me in a dream. She was frightened and distraught, and you know why, don't you?'

'Um, because she is their slave, their prisoner?' said Brahms hopefully.

'Yes,' said Robert, excitedly. 'And who alone can save her, set her free?'

'The handsome prince?' said Brahms, uncertainly.

'Top man!' exclaimed Robert, squeezing his hand. 'Now do you get it?'

Brahms nodded affirmation. Might as well humour him. Aloud, he added with bravura he didn't feel, 'And they will stop at nothing to prevent him coming to the rescue.'

Robert beamed, 'Not even poison,' he whispered. 'That's right. The Seven Dwarves are some of the craftiest poisoners there are.'

Brahms did his best not to gawp.

'And, of course, we all know who their ally is, don't we?'

'The wicked queen?' hazarded Brahms.

'Shush! Here she is,' Robert warned, as the doctor came back into the room. He certainly does look evil, thought Brahms, and that bouffant wig he's adopted really is a bit over the top.

A moment later Clara entered carrying a small carafe of red wine. Drawing a chair up to the bedside, she sat down with incredible poise, dipped a forefinger into the wine and offered it to Robert's parched lips. With closed eyes and the ghost of a smile Robert licked his wife's moistened fingertips. Encouraged, Clara continued the treatment until Robert, overcome with fatigue, finally fell asleep and ceased to respond. Brahms was quite relieved at this. He had found this prolonged pantomime of intimacy disturbingly erotic.

Then, with the exception of the male nurse, they all tiptoed out of the room for a brief conference in the corridor. It was generally agreed that because of Robert's critical condition both Brahms and Clara should stay overnight at the institution, where their every need would be provided for.

But first Clara and Joe decided to walk into Endenich to send a variety of telegrams, after which they partook of a light supper in a local tavern. By the time they got back to the institute it was ten o'clock, and Robert was dead.

TWENTY-ONE

Gossip

THE MANNER OF Robert's passing affected Brahms far more than it did Clara, or so he firmly believed. For instance, she gave little significance to the tale of the Seven Dwarves when Brahms finally got around to recounting it. He, on the other hand, felt that if he had known of his friend's concerns at an earlier date he might well have been able to save his life.

However, the tragedy of it all influenced life in the household far less than he had imagined. Nostalgia has no place in the realms of childhood, and Robert had been gone for more than two years before he died, so he was just a faded memory to most of the kids. And even if he was fresh in the memory of the adults it was their responsibility to give the impression of life going on as usual.

But Marie and Elise were not so easily fooled, as Brahms was to find out one sunny day in August when they cornered him in the garden at lunchtime, as he was enjoying a quiet weissbier and a bratwurst butty. Without ceremony they plonked themselves down at his feet on the grass.

'Have you read this, Joe?' asked Marie, holding up a substantial book.

'We'd like your opinion,' added Elise.

'It's trash,' said Brahms. 'Throw it away. It's an insult to your father's memory. All right, so maybe Robert's symphonies aren't up to the standard of Beethoven's. The man hasn't been born who could equal Beethoven. The writer's an asshole.'

'She called Daddy a second-rate Chopin,' said Elise.

'That's ridiculous,' retorted Brahms. 'They're poles apart.'

'Poles apart – that's funny,' laughed Marie. 'Chopin's a peasant who plays mazurkas and Polish airs; Daddy's music is full of fantasy and the stuff that dreams are made of.'

'She also says that Daddy's madness was caused by an unmentionable social disease,' ventured Elise.

'Exactly what is an unmentionable social disease, Joe?' asked Marie. 'We've never even heard of it.'

'Forget the book. It's crap. Robert's illness was caused by attempting the impossible, like I've told you before. Attempting to express the inexpressible.'

The girls exchanged glances.

'We don't buy it,' said Marie.

'It's bullshit,' added Elise.

Brahms was stymied and took a big bite of his bratwurst and bread to cover his confusion. But the sisters sensed victory and determined to press their advantage. 'When we asked Cook, she said we should ask you,' said Marie.

'She said that if anyone knows, dammit, you should,' said Elise.

'I've warned Cook about encouraging you two to swear. Tell her to mind her own fucking business,' declared Brahms, taking a big swig of beer. 'I'm getting out of here. My life's not my own.'

The girls realized they had overstepped the mark and became contrite.

'You're not thinking of leaving us?' asked Marie.

'You can't. You're like a father to us,' added Elise quickly.

'Yes, a father with no wife,' he snapped.

'We naturally thought that you and Mother . . .' Elise began tentatively.

'Your mother is married to the piano.'

'Until death do them part,' Marie agreed solemnly.

'Amen,' intoned Elise.

'And as it is, tongues are beginning to wag,' said Brahms.

'I've got news for you,' said Marie. 'They've been wagging for months. But we don't mind, do we, sis?'

'Water off a duck's back,' said Elise.

'The longer I stay, the more likely I am to risk compromising your mother's good name. In any case, I've been offered a job as composer-in-residence to the Royal Court in Detmold.'

'Where the hell – I mean, where's Detmold?' demanded Elise.

'Fifty miles south-west of Hanover,' said Brahms. 'In the middle of nowhere.'

'And what will your duties be?' asked Marie.

'To play a few tunes, conduct the choir and instruct the Princess,' said Brahms.

'Oh yes? Instruct her in what, exactly?' She raised an eyebrow.

Brahms racked his brains for a smart rejoinder and was still considering when an upstairs window opened and Clara popped her head out.

'Can you come up a moment, Joe? I need to see you. No rush – when you're finished eating.'

'Coming, darling,' he shouted in relief, prior to taking a last gulp of beer.

The sisters exchanged sly smiles and knowing glances as Brahms raced to obey an order he could not refuse.

TWENTY-TWO

Spoiled for Choice

ETMOLD CAME AND went. Brahms stayed there on and off for three years and got a lot of work done, including a bunch of songs dedicated to a girl he picked up while on holiday in nearby Göttingen. Her name was Agathe Siebold, and they were engaged to be married until Brahms realized that he had no desire as yet to be fettered by the bonds of matrimony and was foolish enough to tell her so. True, there was always the possibility of marriage to his royal pupil Princess Sophie, but with twelve years still to go before she came of age he lacked the patience.

And, try as he might, he could never get Clara out of his mind. He bombarded her with a constant stream of love letters. They made frequent plans to get together, but as demands on her artistry never ceased to flood in she was continually swept away out of reach.

He saw more of the children than the woman of his dreams, despite their being scattered to the four winds. The eldest girls Marie and Elise had been packed off to Gramps for intensive coaching, despite much stamping of feet. Julie had finally escaped from Granny's flat in Berlin, only to be sent off to friends in Switzerland for reasons of health. Ferdy and Ludy had been kicked out of one boarding-school and into another because of the latter's bad behaviour; while little Felix and Eugenie waited at home with Cook for a brief glimpse of a visiting celebrity they were learning to call 'Mummy'. Brahms occasionally dropped by himself, but not as often as he might have.

It wasn't until the summer of 1860 that the long-delayed family holiday actually took place in the little resort of Kreuznach, except for the two schoolboys, that is, who were sent to Gramps for disciplining. So apart from Brahms and young Felix it was largely a female affair – not that either of the young gentlemen was complaining.

By day they all lounged around at picnics or took to the water and were delightfully indolent. In the evening they took it in turns to tuck in nine-year-old Eugenie and little Felix, aged six, and read a bedtime story, then gather for a spritzer in the music room of their rather grand hotel.

Word had quickly got around that Brahms, Clara and at least three of her talented brood were more than likely to entertain each other on the hotel's Bechstein grand, which all agreed was a truly splendid instrument. Thereafter, every seat was taken well before they appeared, except for the places reserved specially for them.

Bit of a busman's holiday, thought Brahms, as he sat down to play. Maybe we should sell tickets. And though he immediately dismissed the notion as daft he was unaware that the same idea had already occurred to Clara, who had far more business acumen than her dear lover. She had sought out the manager and done a deal that resulted in a nice bit of discount, thank you very much. Hell, the hotel was really cashing in on them; people were coming in off the street and staying for supper, yet!

With a flourish Brahms finished his Theme and Variations in D minor and, ignoring the rapturous applause, quickly took his seat next to Clara. He had written it for her and her alone. It was an arrangement of the slow movement of the string sextet he had finished a little over a month ago and was a heartfelt expression of his love for her. He hadn't told her so and felt he had no need to; it was self-evident. The three daughters got it and Mama most certainly got it; and if none of the gawkers got it, many of them did feel its deep emotional pull.

Of course it really needed the rich texture of strings for its full impact to register, and one day Brahms hoped it would be possible to assemble a few friends and treat Clara to a performance all her own. In the meantime he took a private pleasure in knowing she'd certainly enjoy perusing the original score he'd brought along as another billet-doux.

What might the young man have thought if he could have sat in a cinema a hundred years later and heard this very personal piece featured in the famous French film *Les Amants*? Who knows, maybe he did; and maybe a tear or two trickled down his cheek in response.

Back in the hotel music room Marie and Elise treated the appreciative audience to a duet composed by Clara – yes, she, too, was a tunesmith. And finally Julie, whose lung problem had been cleared up by the clean Swiss air, sang one of Brahms's folk songs. In this she was accompanied by her mother, who had planned it as a surprise performance as it was still in manuscript form and had never been played in public.

Brahms was charmed. Naturally, Clara's accompaniment was everything he might have expected and more, but little Julie was a revelation. Not only was her voice incredibly pure, but her performance was very provocative, even sexy. True, the lyrics were a little raunchy. After all, the original peasant version had been about a boy and a girl looking for a needle in a haystack, ending with the girl feeling 'a little prick' . . . Anyway, she made the most of it.

The salacious performance caused Brahms to speculate on the state of her virginity. All right, she was only fifteen years old, but, as every newspaper and journal pointed out almost daily, young girls in mid-nineteenth-century Europe were maturing much faster than a mere decade ago, especially in Berlin, city of vice and decadence.

Brahms was torn between love for the mother and infatuation with the daughter. Then, of course, there were Marie and Elise. He had entertained fantasies of three-in-a-bed sex with them for years, but to be honest their musical skills left him rather cold and caused him to lose interest somewhat. He couldn't think why their performance at the keyboard should dampen his sexual desire, but it most certainly did – dammit!

Oh well, he could still get it on with Clara, thank God. But even as he gave her a good rodgering a few hours later it was cute little Julie he was really mind-fucking.

TWENTY-THREE

Down and Out

BY THE END of the fortnight's holiday it was obvious to most of the family that Brahms was head over heels in lust with Julie. And, quite naturally, most of them were pissed off about it, particularly Elise, who at seventeen had put on puppy fat and earned the sobriquet 'pug dog'.

Marie felt less threatened by her sylph-like rival because, apart from being neat and petite, she had recently come of age and viewed marriage to Brahms as a real possibility. That a burgeoning Julie might beat her to it was too ludicrous to consider. For her the only fly in the ointment was Mother. Though Clara was forty now and well over the hill, she and Joe still went at it hammer and tongs at least three times a week. But Marie had charms of her own. What was that ditty she had heard Cook humming? 'Tight as a drum, never been done, queen of all the virgins.'

No, when it came to a choice between the mare and the filly there would be no contest, she figured. And if Mother objected by pointing out that Joe was hardly in a position to support her, Marie would have a ready answer. 'That's exactly what your father said to you and Daddy, but that didn't stop you two getting spliced, did it? And you weren't even twenty-one, either.'

Yes, Marie had big plans for Joe Brahms, plans of which he was totally unaware.

What of the ageing Clara, what was her position? If Joe had a crush on her third daughter, was it really so different from his getting the measles? In the meantime she was quite content to lie on her back and enjoy her lover's attention, but that was as nothing compared with the bang she got in getting it off on the piano and sending all her admirers into ecstasies. In short, she refused to believe Joe might look elsewhere.

And what did cute little Julie think of it all, when Brahms sneaked a prolonged kiss in the crypt of a baroque church they were sightseeing in? God, how I hate the stink of garlic, she thought.

So what happened after they all said *au revoir* and promised to get together again real soon?

For reasons she kept to herself, Clara made sure the reunion was a long time coming. She found a job for Elise, who was really down in the dumps, as companion to a wealthy widower in Kreuznach, sent Julie to stay with a friend in Munich and took Marie away with her on tour to act as unpaid secretary.

Brahms returned to Hamburg to apply for the post of conductor with the Hamburg Philharmonic, which was just about to fall vacant. But as it happened, the job went to a sober pillar of society. It seems the burghers of Hamburg had long memories.

However, the incident was not without irony, for one Brahms did manage to land a job with the orchestra: Joe's Dad, Jakob. Jakob was a whiz on the cornet, but he also played bass with a small combo down at the local tavern, and it was in this capacity that he was recruited into the ranks of the symphony orchestra. Going from lowbrow to legit was quite a step, and it necessitated constant practice. Though he was tucked well away in the attic, Jakob's wife said it was like being in a sawmill and moved to another part of town, bag and baggage.

And, of course, it was Joe who was left to pick up the pieces.

He'd had it. He too wanted out. He wanted to lose himself in wine, women and song; he wanted to go boating on the beautiful Blue Danube and go waltzing in the Vienna woods. He wanted to shake Johann Strauss by the hand, wish him a big hello and write a few waltzes of his own. He wanted to forget everything to do with family life, let his hair down and shake off the spectre of the Schumanns for good.

TWENTY-FOUR

Here Comes the Bride

I T WAS NINE long years before there was another family get-together, this time at Clara's posh new holiday home in Baden-Baden. The occasion was Julie's wedding – not to Brahms, as might have been expected, but to Count Vittorio Radicati, an Italian widower with two kids.

Brahms was outraged, and even as he knocked at the front door he still entertained the wild idea of talking her out of it. This was despite the fact that he hadn't written her in ages. He had often done so to start with, but since she never replied he had confined his love letters to Clara ever since.

That's not to say he ignored every charmer that crossed his path. Ottilie Hauer was a case in point. Like cute little Julie, she was a great interpreter of his songs, many of which he wrote especially for her. And every time she performed one of his love songs, whether in a private salon or a public concert hall, Brahms felt she was singing to him and him alone, and he was smitten yet again. That voice, those lips, that mouth from which issued the most sensual of sounds were a never-ceasing turn-on, constantly seducing him to erotic daydreams of oral sex down that most divine of deep throats.

Alas, it had soon become clear that this could only be achieved within the bounds of hellish matrimony. He had been sorely tempted but had vacillated month after month, until one snowy Christmas Day, when he confronted her with a wedding ring. He stammered forth a proposal of marriage, only to find she had accepted another suitor just an hour before. So, giving a philosophic shrug, he had popped the ring back in his pocket, found the nearest toilet, had a quick J. Arthur and never looked back. It had been a narrow escape, and – who knows? – the ring might come in handy at a later date . . . which is why it was burning a hole in his trouser pocket at that very moment.

Cook opened the door and seemed pleased to see him. Brahms wondered if she was as foul mouthed as ever. Regardless, he refused her offer to announce him but allowed her to relieve him of his overnight bag. Once inside, he was distracted by the sound of music coming from a room down the hall.

The door was open, so he peered through the crack to see who was making the noise. It was a striking young man of twenty, locked in battle with Clara's baby grand.

Unwilling to become a bystanding casualty, Brahms stepped boldly into the room, causing the performer to practically jump out of his skin and stop playing.

'Uncle Joe! You weren't meant to hear that,' he exclaimed.

'Bravo,' Brahms enthused. 'I've heard Mendelssohn murdered on more than one occasion; you were just inflicting grievous bodily harm. Do me a favour, take up Wagner! By God, you've grown. How many years is it? No, don't tell me. Come on, give me a hug.'

As they embraced, Brahms's mind was racing. Exactly who is this guy, Ludy or Ferdy? He could only hope the truth would out before he could make a complete fool of himself.

'Where is everyone?' said Brahms, hoping for a quick revelation.

'Fussing over the bride,' said the youth.

'Tell me about the groom. Have you met him?'

'No, I've only just arrived myself. But apparently he's very charming, with pots of money.'

'Who else is coming?' asked Brahms, still hoping for a clue to the young man's identity.

'Well, the girls, of course. They're to be bridesmaids. And Felix is to be a pageboy scattering scented rose petals. All very evocative.'

'And how about your other brother?' asked Brahms awkwardly.

'Poor Ludy won't be here. He's been sent off to Gramps for disciplining.'

'Poor fellow!' exclaimed Brahms, safe in the knowledge he was talking to Ferdy.

'All the same, I must say it's heaven without him.'

'I wouldn't wish your grandfather on my worst enemy. It would certainly be a case of the skeleton at the feast if he appeared.'

'We doubt he'll show up,' Ferdy replied. 'After all these years he still hasn't forgiven Mother for marrying against his wishes.'

'Still, you can hardly blame him. As a child prodigy she was his main source of income, which dried up dramatically the minute she married Robert.'

'He was a real skinflint,' confided Ferdy. 'Despite all the money he made out of Clara on those endless tours, he still made her share a room with him.'

'Dirty old man,' leered Brahms, his mind full of dirty pictures.

Further male bonding was interrupted by the sudden arrival of Elise, who had lost her puppy fat and was quite comely now.

'Oh, Uncle Joe, what a lovely surprise,' she exclaimed at the sight of Brahms. 'Ferdy, for heaven's sake, why didn't you say he was here?'

'Cook let him in,' said Ferdy, by way of explanation, as the strangers enjoyed a big hug.

'Oh, it's so good to see you,' enthused Elise.

'Oh, it's so good to feel you,' mimicked Brahms with a wicked wink, ever hopeful.

'You'd better not let my fiancé hear that,' she smilingly admonished.

'What?' gasped Brahms in dismay.

'She's engaged to a rich American,' said Ferdy, putting the boot in.

Brahms felt as if he'd been kicked in the stomach and consequently could only manage a rather breathy 'Congratulations'.

Elise, too, suffered a moment of pause before sensibly changing the subject. 'Well, I was going to fetch Ferdy upstairs to see Julie in all her finery, but in the circumstances it might be easier to bring her down here. Yes, definitely. So both of you wait here. And, Ferdy, play something appropriate.'

As she rushed out Ferdy turned to Brahms for guidance. 'What shall it be, Joe? Wagner or Mendelssohn?'

'Need you ask?' said Brahms with a chuckle, joining him on the bench at the piano.

A moment later an improvised duet based on Mendelssohn's celebrated 'Wedding March' resounded throughout the house, as the bride descended the staircase. So engrossed was Brahms in his performance that he was unaware that Julie had entered the room and didn't catch on until he realized that his partner had stopped playing – in favour of gawping. Brahms, too, was gobsmacked as soon as he turned to take in the bride.

Pow! What Joe saw was a bright shining vision, which metamorphosed into a sublime musical phrase that filled his entire universe – and was suddenly gone, leaving him with nothing but a rather inane smile on his face.

'Charming,' he managed to say, after an enormous effort. 'Charming.'

TWENTY-FIVE

The Morning After

T HE WEDDING DAY had come and gone – and so had Brahms's youth along with it. Or so he felt, as he undressed in the room Julie had only recently vacated, after changing from her bridal gown into her honeymoon trousseau. Her perfume still hung in the air, seemingly to taunt him. Even her dressing-table mirror seemed to mock him as he caught sight of a paunch he could have sworn was definitely not there yesterday.

Yesterday! What a nightmare. All that tempting crumpet dressed in virginal white. Eugenie, just eighteen; Marie, Elise and Julie, still in their twenties; and poor Julie, led like a lamb to the slaughter by that wretched wop ram, old enough to be her father.

Then there was Clara, who had thought it inappropriate to hop into bed together 'before he'd barely shaken the dust off his shoes', as she'd delicately put it. And tonight she just wasn't up for it. Frankly, neither was he, after drowning his sorrows for most of the day, fuck it. And fuck the cook, too. The lazy bitch hadn't changed the sheets, still heavy with Julie's virginal aroma. Oh well, it wasn't the first time he'd resorted to a hand job in moments of female deprivation.

Next morning he just couldn't seem to wash the smell of semen from his hands, and he wondered, as he strummed the piano after breakfast, if he was contaminating the keys.

'What is it?' asked Clara, poking her head around the door.

'Wedding present,' replied Brahms, continuing to play.

'A little late, aren't you?' said Clara. 'She must be back in Milan by now.'

'It's for you,' said Brahms, not looking up.

'Oh, Joe, if this is your subtle way of making yet another proposal,' she said, coming into the room, 'I do wish you'd desist.'

'No, it's not,' said Brahms. 'The moment I set eyes on Julie I gave up on you for good.'

'Yes, I could see you were smitten,' said Clara, taking a seat.

'Alas, I never saw you on your wedding day . . .' he said, trying to face her.

'Well, as you were a child prodigy at the time, playing in the brothels of Hamburg, it's hardly surprising,' she replied.

'But that's how you must have looked,' persisted Brahms.

Clara sensed danger. He was getting sentimental. Let's not dredge up regrets, she thought. Instead, she continued the teasing. 'When the priest said, "If any man knows just cause why these two should not be joined in holy matrimony," I fully expected you to speak up.'

'I was tongue-tied, or I would have,' said Brahms with a smile.

'Well, it's too late now,' said Clara with finality. 'You've missed your chance.' I've missed my chance, too, she thought. I know how it feels. How angry it makes you.

'Who knows, he might die of old age,' said Brahms philosophically.

'You're not exactly a spring chicken yourself,' laughed Clara.

'Seems I can't win,' said Brahms with a sigh. 'Too young for you and too old for Julie.'

'And too poor,' Clara scolded. 'Julie's count has money – though from what I hear your prospects are improving daily, after the huge success of your German Requiem. I was quite surprised.'

'At my huge success,' said Brahms with a laugh.

Clara smiled, shook her head and said, 'Don't be silly. I'm overjoyed. But I thought you were an atheist.'

'I *am* an atheist,' said Brahms proudly. 'A Protestant atheist.'

'That's ridiculous. All your words are taken from the Bible.'

'In Martin Luther's translation.'

'I see what you mean. As far as the Pope is concerned, he's the Devil incarnate.'

'And, as we know, the Devil has all the best tunes,' said Brahms.

'And luckily for us,' chirped Clara, 'the public can't get enough of them.'

'The fact you've taken up my first concerto hasn't done me any harm either. The critics had written it off as a resounding flop.'

'The public love it,' said Clara. She meant it.

A silence of mutual admiration followed, tentatively broken by Brahms.

'Is it really too late for us?' he ventured.

Clara sighed. Too late to trust that love conquers all? Hell, my lover of twenty years is in love with my daughter. And I'm almost too exhausted to care. Aloud she said ruefully, 'You saw what it was like. A concert pianist and a composer living under the same roof: one needs to practise eight hours a day, and the other needs peace and tranquillity. Result: fireworks!' She rubbed her right wrist and mused in silence a while. 'I sometimes wonder if it wasn't my constant practice, practice, practice that finally drove poor Robert . . . to distraction.'

'Nonsense. Your playing has quite the opposite effect. Play something for me now. Play this,' said Brahms, handing her his music.

Clara hesitated, intrigued in spite of herself, as she always was by his music.

Brahms placed the score open on the piano in front of them. 'I wrote it especially for you. Right after I heard about that strained tendon. How is it today?'

'Getting better. If I don't overtax it,' she replied, peering closer to look at the score. What . . . ?

'Which is why I've written this study for the left hand alone, exclusively for you. Play it for me,' said Brahms.

'You are an angel,' whispered Clara She was genuinely moved. He understands. He's the only one who knows I'm afraid . . .

She covered up her feelings, protesting, 'You're not expecting me to sight-read this, are you? It's truly formidable.'

'Well, at least we could try out the tempo,' Brahms suggested.

But Clara was emphatic. 'No! Impossible. Give me ten minutes!'

'Very well,' conceded Brahms. 'I'll go to my room.'

'No, no,' insisted Clara. 'I want you right out of earshot, out of the house. Go take a hike!'

Brahms threw his hands up in surrender. 'I'm gone,' he muttered and left her to it, content that he was back in her good books again. In which case tonight he might get lucky.

TWENTY-SIX

Showdown

HEN BRAHMS RETURNED – three pints and fifty-eight minutes later – it was not to the sound of music but of angry voices. This time it was a worried-looking Ferdy who answered his knock and proffered a brief explanation. 'Marie came across a letter addressed to Mother and read it.'

'So what?' said Brahms.

'It was bad news from Gramps that Mother had been keeping to herself.'

'Was Ludy involved?' asked Brahms, with an uneasy sense of foreboding.

'I certainly heard his name mentioned,' admitted Ferdy.

Feeling a deep sense of unease, Brahms strode down the corridor and listened outside the door of the music room where the row was in progress.

'Presumably, you're not going to stand for it,' said Marie.

'You presume too much, young lady,' snapped Clara. 'Hold your tongue.'

But Marie would not be silenced. 'It's that wretched old man's fault. He was supposed to look after Ludy. He had no right to do that.'

'I left the matter entirely to Father's discretion,' said Clara. 'What he did, he did with my blessing.'

Marie, after years of repression, finally blew her top. 'You coward! You heartless bitch!' she yelled. 'You always make excuses for that depraved martinet! You're just like him!' This was followed by the sound of a loud slap and a scream.

Brahms decided it was time to act and briskly entered the room. 'Has someone seen a mouse?' he quipped rather lamely, referring to the scream.

But Marie was not to be humoured. 'Clara's father has had Ludy committed to the lunatic asylum at Colditz,' she sobbed.

Shocked, Brahms attempted to comfort Marie with a hug, allowing her to cry on his shoulder. 'There's obviously been a mistake. I'm sure your mother will go straight there and sort it out in no time,' said Brahms, looking at Clara.

'There is no mistake, and I will not be going to Colditz. Not yet, anyway. Tomorrow I start a three-month tour,' Clara replied firmly. 'I have important obligations to fulfil.'

'More important than the welfare of your own son?' sobbed Marie accusingly.

'I won't be emotionally blackmailed, young lady,' retorted Clara. 'Better minds than yours have tried it. I am satisfied that Ludy needs treatment. Colditz isn't cheap.'

'It's always about money, isn't it? Proof of your relentless power!'

'And where do you think the money for Colditz will come from? Certainly not from my lady of leisure here,' said Clara with a laugh.

'Who arranges all your tours, collects all your reviews, invests all your money and lives on your charity?' Marie exclaimed vehemently, breaking away from Brahms and facing Clara squarely on. 'Yes, it's me, your "lady of leisure" here, in case you haven't noticed.'

'You know you can always count on me for financial support,' said Brahms, rather ineptly.

'She's rolling in money,' exclaimed Marie, the bit now firmly between her teeth. 'If she never played another note she could still spend the rest of her days in the lap of luxury.'

'You're jealous,' hissed Clara. 'Jealous because you are nothing and I am a star.'

'You're a star, all right,' sneered Marie. 'But you've never shone on us. You relegated us to the outer darkness years ago.'

'Thank you,' said Clara and walked out of the room with what little dignity she could muster.

Marie, drained, collapsed on to the bench. Brahms rested a hand comfortingly on her shoulder.

'Will she ever forgive me?' asked Marie despondently.

'Someone had to say it,' said Brahms.

'I'm so tired,' Marie said with a long-drawn-out sigh. 'Tired of suffering in silence.'

'I know,' said Brahms sympathetically. 'The same could be said for your mother.'

'Mother suffering? Over Daddy, you mean?' suggested Marie.

'I'm sure that not a day goes by that she doesn't relive those last painful hours she spent nursing his poor emaciated body in that awful asylum,' Brahms answered. Marie was old enough to hear this now. 'I saw it, remember. To have kept hopes for him alive so long, silently willing him to return restored, only to be called to say her goodbyes to a shadow.'

'Does that give her the right to abandon poor Ludy?' she asked.

'Don't you see? It would bring it all back to her. She can't face it right now. Just give her time.'

'Then I'll go myself,' said Marie determinedly.

This took Brahms by surprise. 'You can't possibly go.'

'And why not?'

Brahms had to think quickly. He had to protect Marie. Colditz was notorious. Just the sight of it was enough to inspire dread. She would never survive it. 'Well, for one thing Clara needs your support on the tour.'

'I thought you were on my side,' said Marie heatedly.

'I am. Of course I am. But what with that strained tendon and the stress of the wedding and the problem of Ludy, she needs help. She needs *you*, sweetie, don't you see? She's more fragile than she admits. And don't worry. I'll visit Ludy myself, talk to him man to man. I was planning on leaving today anyway,' he lied.

'She hates me,' said Marie simply.

'Hates you? Hates the one person who makes her life bearable? You're indispensable. Believe me, she adores you.' He hugged her for emphasis.

Well, if she believes that she'll believe anything, thought Brahms, as Marie kissed him goodbye on the front porch. And as he made his way alone to the station he thought, What a disastrous visit. No Julie, no Clara, no anything. Nothing to look forward to but a dismal journey to meet yet another mad member of the family.

'Get a life, Joe,' he shouted into the night. 'For Christ's sake, get a life!'

TWENTY-SEVEN

Veterans

*T*WENTY YEARS PASSED before Brahms set foot in Baden-Baden again. The occasion was Clara's seventieth birthday, and by now he was just about the most famous living composer on the face of the earth. Shaking off his obsession with the Schumann family seemed to have opened the floodgates of creativity. He was hailed as a worthy successor to Beethoven; in fact, his first symphony had been hailed as 'Beethoven's Tenth', because of the use of a theme Brahms had borrowed from the Master. Regardless of this, he was very much his own man, with a voice quite unique in the world of music that was accessible to the layman and lords and ladies alike. Could he be running a risk in renewing his old association with the Schumann circus?

Years and years ago Robert had predicted the 'Age of the Three Bs – Bach, Beethoven and Brahms', and, lo and behold, his prediction had come to pass. Brahms, too, had also become associated with 'three B's' of his own, 'beer, beard and belly'. Yes, the dapper young man who had first knocked on the Schumanns' back door thirty-seven years previously had become a portly, eccentric, untidy sort of fellow, almost down-at-heel.

Cook didn't recognize him at first and was about to tell him to go around to the tradesmen's entrance, when just in time she recognized his voice. 'No, Madame Clara's not in at the moment,' she replied in answer to his question, 'but Master Ferdinand's about, so do come in and let me take that heavy bag.'

Brahms voiced his thanks and, as the door closed behind him, was smitten by an overwhelming sense of *déjà vu*. That piano music coming from a room at the end of the hall had a very familiar ring to it. As before, he peered through a crack in the door – this time to see a rather seedy middle-aged man labouring over Schumann's Carnavale. Brahms recognized him as Ferdy, more by his heavy-handed piano-playing than by his appearance.

'Still murdering the classics, I see,' said Brahms with an air of joviality as he burst into the room.

'Hi, Joe. Good to see you. How goes it?' Ferdy said, jumping to his feet and shaking Brahms by the hand.

'Fine, thank you.' Brahms replied. 'Where is everyone?'

'Her courtiers, what's left of them, are all dancing attendance on the Queen Mother.'

'You are referring to the birthday girl, I imagine?'

'She's getting a medal from His Majesty, the Kaiser.'

'For valiant service to Kaiser and country, I presume, and about time, too.'

'A gold medal,' emphasized Ferdy.

'Which she has won victoriously in the bloody battle of the keyboards. A veteran if ever there was one.'

'Pity His Majesty wasn't so generous to the veterans of the real war,' said Ferdy with a hint of bitterness.

'I heard about your illness,' said Brahms softly.

'Mother told me you offered financial help to the wife and kids when I was hospitalized.'

'I was sorry when Clara turned me down, but she's a proud woman. She won't accept charity.'

'Not even on behalf of others,' Ferdy replied bitterly.

'Come now, she's been pretty generous to you. Own up.'

'Oh, she'll pay any amount of money to have you locked up,' said Ferdy with mock cheerfulness. 'Look at poor Ludy. He's been in Colditz for close on twenty years.'

'Actually it's over twenty years. And to tell you the truth I was rather surprised to find you here. When did the authorities discharge you from the clinic?'

'I discharged myself yesterday,' said Ferdy with a hint of bravado. 'I'm cured, "rehabilitated".'

'What does Clara say?' asked Brahms.

'She doesn't know. Cook let me in. Surprise birthday present. I'm here to drink her health.'

So saying, Ferdy reached for a glass of amber liquid on top of the piano, raised it, took a sip and replaced it, whereupon Brahms snatched it up and took a sip himself. Horrible! He quickly spat it out and poured the rest into a handy potted plant. Outraged, Ferdy clenched his fists and for a moment seemed as if he'd strike Brahms.

'It seems you've given up one drug only to take up another,' said Brahms accusingly.

'I've got toothache,' said Ferdy defensively. 'I found it upstairs in the medicine cabinet.'

'Opium, isn't it?'

'Chloral. They give it to fretful babies.'

'Poor bastards,' muttered Brahms.

A short, painful silence followed, broken by the sound of voices at the front door. Then footsteps sounded down the hall, heralding Clara's turbulent entrance into the room. A storm threatened, which Brahms cleverly forestalled by breaking into song:

> Happy birthday to you, happy birthday to you,
> Happy birthday, dear Clara, happy birthday to you.

One glance at Ferdy and Marie, who had also appeared, was enough to get them joining in, and by the time they had all sung a couple of verses the sting had gone out of Clara's waspish attitude. Directly the song ended Brahms rushed up to Clara and covered her face with kisses, causing her to laugh in spite of herself.

'Joe, stop! You're drowning me,' she cried.

'A kiss for every year of your life!' Brahms jokingly persisted.

'Up to the age of twenty-one,' Marie added, diplomatically.

'. . . eighteen, nineteen, twenty, twenty-one. There!' he counted as he kissed her, and before she could catch her breath he continued his onslaught. 'And here, close to my heart, a very personal birthday present.' From an inside jacket pocket he produced a rolled-up manuscript and handed it to Clara with a flourish.

'Mmm, it's still warm,' she purred, holding it to her cheek momentarily before she unscrolled it. Her face fell. 'Piano Sonata No. 3 in F minor,' she read. 'Have you forgotten so soon?'

'So soon?' replied Brahms, rather bemused. 'It must be over forty years since you first set eyes on it.'

'Not as long as that, surely,' she replied, aghast.

'This is a brand new version, completely revised and, I might add, nowhere near as demanding,' said Brahms.

Then Clara flicked through a few pages and stopped to read an inscription:

'"Night falls and the moon shines.
Two loving hearts are united,
Embracing each other blissfully."'

'Well, the quotation at the head of the second movement certainly hasn't changed,' she continued.

'No, the meaning hasn't changed at all, even if the notes have. Listen, tell me what you think.' And he propped up the music on the piano and started to play.

But Clara was unable to remain silent. 'There you go, Joe, with your irrepressible banging and thumping. A more apt quote would have been "Love lies bleeding",' she said dismissively, and elbowing Brahms aside she continued to play where he'd left off.

The difference was revelatory, as Brahms had hoped it would be.

And as Clara continued to work her magic, Brahms gave a nod to Marie, who handed Ferdy his crutches and helped him quietly from the room, closing the door softly behind her. Brahms was in heaven.

TWENTY-EIGHT

Two Loving Hearts

*T*HERE WERE TEARS in Brahms's eyes when Clara finally lifted her hands from the keyboard and rested them in her lap like two magic birds come to rest after a sonic flight of enchantment.

Brahms knelt at Clara's feet and kissed the palm of each hand and then the backs of each hand and every individual finger and thumb. If it had been at all possible, he would also have kissed the soul that had given his music such vibrant life. What he had written was a love song without words, and what he had just heard was a reading that reflected his most intense feelings a hundredfold.

'Are you absolutely certain there is no hope for us?' said Brahms, gently resting his head on her lap.

As Clara carefully considered her reply, she softly and slowly stroked his hair – which unfortunately did not prepare Brahms for the finality of her answer.

'We have just experienced what few mortals can ever aspire to – the bliss of a perfect marriage,' she said, in almost a whisper. 'The ultimate communion of souls, never to be repeated, but eternally treasured. Anything further could be nothing but a painful memory.'

'I take it that's a no,' said Brahms, deeply hurt, as he rose abruptly to his feet.

'I shall never play it again,' said Clara evenly.

'Don't worry, there're plenty who will,' he replied bitterly.

'I haven't played the piece for some time,' she went on. 'The original music, that is. It's unbearably sad.'

'What do you mean?' asked Brahms, genuinely puzzled.

'Not the music itself but the associations that come with it.'

'I see what you mean,' said Brahms, reflecting on his present state of mind. I'm in love with a woman I can't possess.'

'What has just passed between us only confirms my resolve. But I was referring to the occasion when I performed it at a recital, a few hours after Julie died.'

Here she paused, giving Brahms a moment to consider the hurt he, too, had felt all those years ago and which had never left him. How long ago was it? It seemed a lifetime. November 1872. My God, it's been seventeen years.

Further reflection was cut short when Clara continued to reminisce. 'Poor Julie, one pregnancy after another, in her delicate state of health. How I despise that heartless man. The evening of her death I played as never before. The audience was in tears. There were those who said I was heartless not to have cancelled the concert, that I should have sat at the bedside with the corpse. But I preferred to cherish Julie's spirit with music. I left Marie to keep vigil. She has a more conventional sense of duty.'

'You can always depend on good old reliable Marie to do the right thing,' said Brahms by way of conversation, his mind preoccupied with his own memories.

But Clara did not appreciate the spotlight being redirected. 'Oh, she's far from infallible, believe me. I shall never forget her insensitive behaviour the night Felix died, after a long fight against TB, poor soul. It's incredible! My baby boy! I was sleeping only next door and she failed to wake me. Unforgivable!'

'I'm sure there was a reason,' Brahms protested lamely.

'Oh, she had a reason all right. Knew I'd had a tiring recital that evening and "didn't want to disturb me". What nonsense!'

'She's thoughtful to a fault,' said Brahms, mindful he was in a no-win situation.

'When I finally got to see him,' replied Clara bitterly, 'he was stiff and cold. I shall never forget those wide, reproachful eyes. How was he to know, poor darling?' And she stared at Brahms for sympathy – which he had a problem formulating. Easy to mourn after they're gone, but to love while they live . . . ?

In any event, he was saved by the sudden arrival of Marie, who looked as if her ears were burning.

'Supper's ready,' she announced. 'Don't let it get cold.'

Good ol' Marie.

TWENTY-NINE

Guilt

BRAHMS CUT HIMSELF a slice of bread, wrapped it around a sliver of Münster cheese, dipped it into his glass of hock and took a big juicy bite.

Clara had left most of her food uneaten and seemed to be studying the prismatic effect of candlelight on crystal, her lips pressed tight together.

'Well, if you'll excuse us, we have work to do,' said Marie, giving Ferdy a gentle kick beneath the table.

'Oh, yes,' he responded, getting the message.

'Work at this time of night?' queried Brahms.

'We've got a fresh batch of press clippings for the scrapbook,' said Marie. 'Ferdy's a dab hand with the paste pot, aren't you, love?'

'Glad to be of use,' said Ferdy, gathering up his crutches as his sister collected the dirty plates.

When they had left the couple alone, the awkward silence that had characterized the meal was broken by Brahms. 'What do you intend to do about Ferdy? I had no idea he was a virtual cripple.'

'A painful legacy of the war,' replied Clara coldly. She still had not forgiven Ferdy for absconding from the clinic and turning up unannounced. 'That's why they put him on drugs in the first place, to combat the pain. After that it was a short step to addiction.'

Brahms thanked his lucky stars he had never been tempted, though drugs were readily available to all in every apothecary's shop throughout the land.

'I'm in two minds about his future,' Clara continued. 'I could send him back for further treatment, but that's expensive, or I could let him stay here. With Ludy at Colditz, Eugenie at the Academy and Elise raising a family in America, Marie has virtually nothing to do – apart from planning my tours, of course.'

'And keeping a scrapbook of your rave reviews,' said Brahms with a touch of cynicism. 'With Ferdy to lend a helping hand.'

'A little beneficial therapy will do him the world of good,' said Clara, with no hint of irony.

'And Marie can proudly add the role of nurse to her curriculum vitae,' said Brahms. 'What a paragon, and pretty with it.'

'Now then,' said Clara. 'Don't get any ideas. She's taken.'

'Yes, by you!' Brahms sensed he was talking himself into trouble and changed tack. 'Christ, how I wish I'd taken Julie. She'd still be alive today.'

'Away with you,' sneered Clara. 'It would practically have been incest. By the way, did you remember my old love letters?'

'Yes.'

'Can I have them?'

'Yes.' Brahms didn't like the way things were going and dunked the remains of his sandwich into the wine and stuffed it into his mouth.

'Can I have them?' said Clara again, reaching for the nutcracker.

'Yes,' mumbled Brahms, his mouth full of bread.

'Now. I'd like them now,' said Clara, cracking a walnut.

'This very minute? Why?' he said in an effort to swallow.

'They might fall into the hands of some unscrupulous biographer who'd exploit them. Give people the wrong impression.'

'The impression we were lovers, you mean,' replied Brahms coldly, rising to his feet.

'We have our reputations to consider,' said Clara, popping the crushed nut into her mouth.

Clearly hurt, Brahms left the room and went in search of his Gladstone bag. He found it in Julie's old room. Memories, memories and still more memories as he rummaged through his belongings for the letters. There were two bundles to choose from. The first one turned out to be some gems from his correspondence with Ludy in Colditz. As he foraged through them, he felt guilty. It had been some time since he'd last written to the poor man and longer still since his last visit – much longer. Why did his every association with the family evoke feelings of guilt? He was sick of it. Would it never end? But he only had himself to blame. His agony was to a large extent self-inflicted.

He chose instead the myriad watersilk envelopes with their postmarks from every country, addressed to him in Clara's perfectly precise script with its

curling flourishes. What a cargo of ardour they hid. About to be jettisoned . . .
Well, the main thing was the present moment, wasn't it? What did it matter
that she'd once thrown herself at him in rather purple prose? Like this, for
instance . . . Let's see. Brahms took a near-transparent leaf from its sheath.

> If you enter a room where I'm playing, and my cheeks are slightly flush and
> damp with effort, know yourself to have kindled the blaze which burns
> fiercely on the keyboard and even then between my thighs, whose path I
> trace always with slavish fingers, unable to extinguish the heat, the relent-
> lessly searing rhythm . . . while the audience hears only my precision and
> mistakes it for delicacy.

Hmm. Not bad to have been the cause of such a fever, and in such a con-
trolled temperament as hers. Oh well. So she's fearful of her legacy. Wouldn't
do for the world to discover their aloof Grand Dame of Keyboard Purity was a
rutting schoolgirl at heart, once and always.

On returning to Clara he tossed the rather large bundle on the table where
she was still cracking nuts with an almost manic compulsion.

Pausing for a moment, she stared at the ancient letters but didn't touch
them. 'How romantic,' she finally said, deprecatingly. 'All tied up with greasy
string. That's how I keep my old butcher's bills.'

'Quite fitting, don't you think?' replied Brahms, raising his voice. 'Considering they're a complete load of tripe. And what have you done with mine?'

'Burned them along with the rubbish, years ago,' she almost shouted.

Marie was standing at the door. They both noticed her at the same time
and froze. 'Do you remember what Daddy used to say whenever there was
fighting over a bone of contention?' she said placidly. The two antagonists
remained silent, prompting Marie to continue. 'Bury it,' she said, simply.

'. . . and let the grass grow over it,' said Clara, sighing as she remembered.

'. . . or, better still, flowers,' Brahms added, also recalling the words of his
long-dead friend.

That night Brahms and Clara went to bed together for the last time and
slept chastely in each other's arms, like children.

THIRTY

Epilogue:
The Angel of Death

THE MUSIC ROOM was deserted but by no means empty. A familiar presence, hidden as it was under a black silk shawl, still dominated the familiar space. Yes, it was Robert Schumann's gift to his young fiancée on the occasion of their engagement – the hand-painted baby grand piano, that long-cherished instrument that had only recently yielded to his beloved's touch for the last time.

Voices in the hall pre-empted the appearance of Marie and Brahms, she in mourning, he in travelling clothes and holding a Gladstone bag. At the sight of the piano draped in funereal black, Brahms hastily removed his hat. For a moment their animated conversation halted, as Brahms paid his respects.

Marie hurried on, apologetically. 'We waited and waited, but we couldn't delay the service for ever. Did you miss your connection or what?'

'Worse,' he sighed. 'I caught a train travelling in the wrong direction.'

'Oh, Joe, you poor dear, you must be exhausted. Do sit down, please.'

As Brahms collapsed into a big armchair he tried to make light of the sombre situation. 'This is becoming a habit. Poor Ferdy, I missed his funeral, too. Was it drugs?' He could have kicked himself – he hadn't meant to broach the subject.

'An overdose,' she replied. 'Let's have a drink.'

'Thank you, my dear. Not for me. Doctor's orders. I shouldn't even be here. Complete rest and all the nonsense that goes with it, you know. Fuss, fuss, fuss.'

Marie did her best not to look worried as he rambled on.

'I was to have conducted the Fourth Symphony in Vienna next week, but now he's forbidden it, the wretch, and I've had to cancel. I'm virtually a prisoner in my own house. Awful!'

'Awful,' replied Marie. 'I know very well how you feel. I sympathize.' And what an understatement that turned out to be.

'Are you all alone here now?' asked Brahms, not wishing to discuss his ill health further.

'All, all alone,' said Marie wistfully. 'Eugenie was the last to go, following in Mama's illustrious footsteps. She's making quite a name for herself. And, luckily for her, it's a name that commands considerable respect, particularly in England, though I doubt she'll top Clara's record of twenty-three grand tours.'

'Tell me,' said Brahms, getting down to the nitty-gritty. 'I've been meaning to ask. Clara, how did she . . . I mean, did she . . . ?'

'No, she didn't suffer,' said Marie, putting him out of his misery. 'This time last year she was still giving recitals, aged seventy-five. Then she had that stroke, from which she never fully recovered, poor dear. Those songs you wrote were a great comfort to her; she wanted you to know that. She was most insistent. "Marie, promise me! You must, must, must remember. And if you do forget, I shall never, never forgive you!"'

Brahms noticed Marie was smiling, prompting him to smile in return. 'A request you dare not refuse,' he said.

'She died peacefully in my arms at sunset,' Marie continued, tears welling in her eyes. 'Yes, peacefully in my arms.' But the emotional strain of not only the last few days but an entire life dedicated to the well-being of others, aggravated by the joy and fulfilment she had only ever experienced second hand, finally overspilled in a torrent of grief. 'Died peacefully in my arms,' she repeated, almost in hysterics. 'Peacefully in my arms, arms that have only known the embrace of death.' At this she turned to Brahms with a look of accusation, or at least that's how he took it. 'Only the embrace of death, Joe, never once the embrace of love.'

With some considerable effort, Brahms hoisted his generous bulk from the armchair and embraced Marie with a clumsy bear hug. 'That's not so, Marie,' he protested. 'How many of us are fortunate enough to die enveloped in such a profound, all-embracing love as yours? You are love personified. I only hope you are near when my turn comes.'

Then he did something he had been sorely tempted to do for years: he kissed her passionately on the lips. 'You are an angel,' he whispered in her ear, pressing her ever tighter until she took the initiative and began pushing him gently away.

'Yes, I am an angel all right,' she said with a glitter of fear in her eyes. 'My name is Asrael.'

Brahms looked blank, not being so well versed in Oriental mythology as the old friend he still deeply cherished.

'Asrael?' he questioned.

'The Angel of Death,' she pronounced.

At this Brahms shuddered involuntarily but clung to her ever tighter. Marie gave the softest of sighs and abandoned herself to his trembling embrace.

In less than a year, Joe Brahms was dead . . .

. . . But his music lives on eternally.